SPIES
WANTED

SPIES
WANTED

LONNIE SPIVAK

MILL CITY PRESS

Mill City Press, Inc.
2301 Lucien Way #415
Maitland, FL 32751
407.339.4217
www.millcitypress.net

Edited by Chris Roberts, Jeff McMahon

Printed in the United States of America

ISBN-13: 978-1-54566-574-9

TABLE OF CONTENTS

Special thanks to my wife Staci, and Daughters Gillian and Lexi for putting up with all of my crazy ideas. I love you all.

CHAPTER 1

JEANIE MILLER

"Jeanie. Jeanie. *Jeanie!*" This was all she heard as her science teacher, Mr. Jennings, woke her from a daydream. It was late in the school day, and the class was learning about basic physics. "Jeanie, would you mind telling the class about the basics of Einstein's Theory of Special Relativity?" Jeanie was looking with a blank stare out the window overlooking the main entrance of the school. Mr. Jennings chose to emphasize the word *basics*, as Jeanie had a tendency to go on and on with great detail about most every subject. He knew that it would be much easier to get her to explain this to the class than to try to do it himself. Mr. Jennings had been teaching for more than thirty years; he was yearning for retirement, and he really didn't want to be bothered if he could help it. "Earth to Jeanie...*hello*?" Mr. Jennings continued.

It was late spring, and it was getting harder and harder for Jeanie to pay attention. She was looking forward to the end of the school year and ready to take a well-deserved vacation, far away from the snickering know-nothings who surrounded her at this school.

Jeanie blinked a couple of times and stood up as she returned to reality. After a couple of seconds, she said, "Uh...okay." The class snickered behind her yet again. "The Special Theory of Relativity was introduced in Albert Einstein's 1905 paper 'On the Electrodynamics of Moving Bodies.' It basically said that nothing could move faster than the speed of light. It also led to the development of the atomic bomb with the now-infamous equation of mass–energy equivalence:

$$E = mc^2$$

or energy equals mass times acceleration squared."

Jeanie continued. "However, recent tests conducted in an underground proton accelerator and collider showed that the subatomic neutrino particles can move faster than light. This discovery will change our understanding of physics and Einstein's Theory of Special Relativity. It also opens the door for the development of faster-than-light or warp drives." Her thoughts raced and she was about to continue before she was interrupted by Mr. Jennings.

"Okay, okay...thank you Jeanie," he said. As she sat back down, she heard the usual giggles and returned to her daydream.

Jeanie Miller was a twelve-year-old overachiever, with sandy-brown hair and blue eyes. Her parents knew early on that she was different from other kids. She absorbed every-thing around her and instantly seemed to under-stand the inner workings of whatever it was she was doing at the time. By the time she turned two, Jeanie was already reading at a fourth-grade level. At six, she became a member of MENSA, an organization of those people with the highest IQ's from all over the world. Later that same year, she received national attention for her exceptional abilities in math and science.

Her genius, however, kept her isolated from everyone, including her peers as well as most adults. Her teachers felt threatened because Jeanie understood more about their subjects than the teachers ever would; her classmates treated her like a freak and often teased her about her age, size, intellect... and pretty much anything else they could target. As a result, Jeanie had few, if any friends. So, she did what every young genius would do...

She invented them.

Jeanie's imagination would carry her to other times and faraway worlds. She really considered these to be her current life in alternate dimensions based on String Theory, through which multiple dimensions exist in the same space, with each dimension being different than the next it touches. During these fantasies, Jeanie would bring her imaginary friends on the adventures of a lifetime to the fringes of what is known and possible with current technology.

It was her imagination that kept Jeanie from graduating high school by the time she was ten. In fact, Jeanie probably could have graduated any college she chose already, but her parents just didn't feel that Jeanie was grounded enough with the maturity needed to attend a university. Jeanie would often say, "I don't really want to go to college. I don't think it would be any different than high school; the kids would just be older."

Now that the school year was ending, Jeanie was even more distracted than usual. She sat in class, staring blankly, lost deep in her own thoughts, barely listening to what the teacher was saying. She became more distant as she looked forward to summer break.

Sometimes Jeanie would ponder what she would do if she were only *normal*; the rest of the time, she created the most elaborately detailed stories for herself. Some of her stories were so far-fetched, one might expect them to be the next Hollywood blockbusters.

Jeanie accepted her outcast status, but she wasn't happy about it. She longed for a time she would be able to make friends her own age. Every day when she would get home from school, her mom would ask, "So, what did you do today?"

Usually, Jeanie would just reply, "Nothing." But once in a while, she would come up with details from one of her alternate dimensions about how she saved the world … or something. When she really got going, her mother would just nod occasionally as if she were really listening to what Jeanie was saying. Jeanie would soon realize she had lost her mom's attention and would quietly sneak away to her bedroom to work on her latest invention.

Being a pre-teen is *hard*. At twelve, you're not old enough to be taken seriously by grown-ups, and you're in a real awkward stage developmentally. For Jeanie, being a genius just made it all the more difficult. She just wasn't comfortable telling her mom the truth about how the other kids made her feel, so instead, she would try to rationalize away what made her feel different.

I'm not the prototypical geek. I'm a grown-up in a small body. Maybe I'm remembering information from past lives, she would often think to herself. *If I am reliving a past life, whose life am I reliving? Was I a genius in that life, too? Did I find a way to project my consciousness through space and time?*

Jeanie's mother was a stay-at-home mom to Jeanie and her two-year-old brother, Mikey. But before she had children, Sarah Miller was a nuclear physics professor at Temple University. She had a slender build, reddish-blonde hair and a kind disposition which seemed to balance her husband's impatience and quick-temper. Jeanie looked up to her mom, but she never really understood why her mom gave up her profession to raise a family. Even so, Jeanie was happy to find a friendly face waiting at home for her every day after school, for those times she felt like talking about her day.

Jeanie and her family lived in a typical middle-class home in Virginia, just outside Washington, DC. The house was more than one hundred years old, but it had been remodeled in recent years. The two-story red brick home was beautiful, with white columns outside the front door and an arched window over the entrance. There were old oakwood floors with plenty of space for everyone, and the kitchen had been updated before the Millers moved in. Overall, they lived in a nice house with a better-than-average family atmosphere.

Jeanie had begun to accept her life when her father, Steve, came home that day in May and changed everything. He walked through the door in his usual heavy manner; he was a big man, and every step he took seemed to be with a *thud*.

"Hey!" he yelled, as he dropped his keys on the table by the door. "Everyone! Get down here; I've got some news!"

Jeanie shot down the stairs with anticipation. *I wonder what it is?* she thought to herself, imagination flying. It took only a few seconds for her to get down the stairs. She had already decided that it had something to do with his job, since he just got home and wanted to tell everyone some *news*.

Jeanie's dad, Steve Miller, worked for NewG-Tech (NGT). NGT was a company with a defense contract to build military weaponry, and provide intelligence materials to the government. Steve was being relocated to the plant in the Denver area to supervise the development of a new GPS (global positioning system) component for an unmanned spy plane. His work was classified, but he often talked with Jeanie about the projects he had in development. Because Steve often consulted with Jeanie, she was listed as a Freelance Consultant by NGT... which included a low-level classified clearance that allowed her to discuss plans and programs with her father without him going to jail for sharing classified secrets. Her ability to look beyond the obvious made her a valuable asset. Jeanie liked this time with her father, and the connection they shared definitely made her a daddy's girl. He was one of the few people on earth she felt *understood* her.

This was a unique arrangement; not even Jeanie's mom could discuss most of Steve's work. The Pentagon knew it was a risk giving Jeanie this responsibility, but they didn't want to squander her genius. As a result, she had her own bank account and plenty of her own spending money. While she would spend some of it on clothes or an occasional electronic component, she saved most of her money ... as she had no real social life requiring it.

Once the whole family was gathered around Steve in the living room, he rubbed his hands together, nervously searching for the right words.

"Well...umm," he stammered. Jeanie's mom already knew that what was coming was not going to be good. Her eyes narrowed and she waved her right hand back and forth, prodding him.

"Come on, spit it out already," she sighed.

"Well, I, uh…see, well, we're being relocated," he said. The relief on his face was evident … once he finally got the words out. "At the end of the school year, we're moving to Lakewood, Colorado. I've been asked to head up the continued development of this project Jeanie and I have been working on. And, well, they are moving us to a new facility in Colorado.

Jeanie's face turned bright red, and she focused on her dad with eyes that seem to bore through him like laser beams. She tried not to just totally lose her composure as she clenched her teeth together and mumbled in a tight-lipped way. "I can't believe you are going to make me go through all of this! What if I won't go?"

"Jeanie, unfortunately, we really don't have a choice," her dad said reservedly. "We all have to go. This is a classified program, and I have a contract … which means I *have to* complete this project. You know you're a valuable member of my team, and I can't do it without you."

"Aaauuurrgghh!" Jeanie screamed, turning quickly to run upstairs and slamming the door to her room. She jumped on her bed and buried her head in her pillow.

Her mind started to race as she clamored for images of what things might be like in Colorado, as she turned her focus from the status quo.

Sarah was not pleased either. As Jeanie stormed out, Sarah motioned in a serious manner for her husband to join her in the kitchen for what he knew would not be a pleasant encounter. He had struggled to find the best way to deliver the bad news, but decided that ripping the Band-Aid off quickly was the best way to get the least pushback and resentment.

Steve and Sarah had been married for almost twenty years. At first, they were not sure if they even wanted to have kids. They were both successful in their careers and happy with the freedom they had without children. They put off starting a family for five years, but eventually

Sarah decided the time had come. Not long after that, Jeanie was born.

Sarah tried not to raise her voice as she said, "Don't I have a say in this?" She knew she didn't … and really, neither did Steve. When NGT said, "You're moving," you had to move. When you do classified work for the government, it's just part of the deal.

Steve gently grabbed her hand and looked her in the eyes. They were still very much in love. "Babe, I know you're mad, but you know this is out of my hands," he said. "On the upside, I hear they have a huge house all ready and waiting for us."

"I really wish they would consult us before turning our lives upside down," said Sarah, resigning.

"NGT looks at us as *assets*; to them, we don't have personal lives," grumbled Steve. "It's all about the project, completing it on time and on budget. We've really been lucky, through the years, that we really have not had to relocate more."

Sarah looked up at her husband with puppy-dog-eyes, nodded and said, "I know, but that doesn't mean I have to like it. I really wish there were other options." She paused for a minute and said, "Let's go out for dinner. I don't feel like cooking anymore."

With that, the conversation was over – and preparations for the big move were underway.

For Jeanie, once the initial shock of the impending move wore off, she felt more excited than scared. This was the only place she had ever called home, but the thought of starting over gave her a sense of hope. She imagined she was joining the Witness Protection Program, and her past could be a secret. She imagined making friends…friends *her own age*. Her mind raced as she fantasized about her future. "When I get a chance, I'm going to research Lakewood," she thought to herself. "I might as well know as much about the area as possible."

"Jeanie! *Jeanie!* Come on down. We're going to grab some dinner," Sarah yelled up the stairwell.

Jeanie really did not feel like getting up, but her stomach was rumbling. Not wanting to let the current emotional trauma go to waste, she was ready for a good and expensive dinner. "Can we get some steak?" she asked in her pitiful, *please, Daddy* voice. She knew this was his weakness as she looked up at him with sad eyes. With that look on her face, he couldn't say no, especially to a good steak.

"Sure," he said. "I'll grab your brother."

Jeanie's brother, Mikey, was quite a bit younger than her. At two years old, he was quite a handful with all the energies of a toddler boy. Sarah often said, "Even in the womb, he was high-energy ... always kicking and squirming around." In fact, they often called him "Mr. Squirmy."

It took about ten minutes for the family to pile in to Sarah's minivan, and they were off to dinner. The ride to the restaurant was quiet. Jeanie and her mother both had the same blank look on their faces as they both were lost in deep thought while Mikey just sat in his car seat, oblivious to the major life changes the family was about to embrace.

Sitting at the restaurant, there was an uncomfortable silence. Jeanie piddled on her phone while Sarah tended to Mikey. Steve sat contemplating all of the preparing that would need to be done, wondering if this move was really the best thing for them all. It wasn't long before the waiter brought their food. Jeanie's parents didn't make much eye contact during dinner, and when they were all finished, they piled back into the minivan and headed home.

Back at the house, Jeanie went to her room and reviewed the afternoon's upheaval. She weighed all of the pros and cons in her head, over and over, until finally tiptoeing down the stairs to find her mom and dad snuggled up on the couch, watching some cop show on TV.

She wiggled her way in-between them and laid her head on her dad's shoulder. "Dad," she said. "I want you to know that I'm okay with moving. Maybe this will help me find some kids my own age that I can hang out with." Steve leaned in to give his big girl a kiss as they had a family hug on the couch.

CHAPTER 2

THE BIG MOVE

F or the next few weeks, Jeanie went through her typical routine as she waited for the school year to end. She would wake up early, head down to make some toaster waffles, pull out her laptop to look over the latest tech blogs and any messages from her dad. She would then breeze through her school day.

After arriving back at home, she would tinker on gadgets in her room or work on whatever tasks her dad had for her. Her mom would insist she stop for dinner … but she would start the routine all over the following day. At this pace, it wasn't long before Jeanie was out of school for the summer, and before she knew it, the time had come to pack up and leave the only home she had ever known.

It was around 6:00am when the movers showed up in the driveway. Steve went out to greet them as the driver exited the van. "Good morning, sir," the driver said in a cordial but sturdy voice.

"Good...yeah, I guess," Steve replied. "I'm not really looking forward to this move, and the wife and kids have already given me enough grief."

"I understand, sir, but we'll do our best to make this a painless process," said the mover.

"I appreciate that."

"Before we can get started, I need to verify your identification," said the driver, pulling a clipboard from the van. "Can I see your NGT ID and driver's license?"

"Sure," Steve replied as he reached into his pocket to pull out his wallet. He opened it up, showed the driver his license, then dug into one of the credit card slots for his NGT ID.

"Thank you sir. Can you give me your security code for verification?" The driver scrawled onto the clipboard.

"My code is *9764Juno*. Anything else?"

"No sir, we'll take it from here," said the driver, tossing the clipboard back onto the dashboard. He motioned to the rest of his crew to get out of the van, and the movers gathered by the passenger door of the van for their instructions.

With that, the big move was underway and the Miller family watched as the contents of their house were packed up by the moving company that handles all of NGT's employees' relocations. Room-by-room, the four men moved meticulously, carefully logging every item as they went along.

Jeanie watched the men as they moved with military precision. Even though the moving truck said *United Movers*, they were all members of the military and had a certain level of security clearance, which allowed them to see and move classified materials. This was required because of the nature of Steve's work. The men all dressed as typical movers - jeans and a company shirt - but each was exceptionally well-groomed, with a muscular build and military haircut.

"What's your rank?" Jeanie asked the men one by one, as she tried to not think about moving.

"I'm First Sergeant Singer," one of the men replied. "You guys seem to have a lot of stuff."

"Well … you know, we like our gadgets," said Jeanie, trying not to look to upset about the move as she followed Sergeant Singer from room to room.

"How did you know we were military?" Sergeant Singer asked.

"Well, I figured they couldn't just send any out-of-the-blue moving company to move my dad's stuff. The way you greeted my dad, and you're pretty put together for movers."

Singer cracked a smile as he looked down at Jeanie. "I guess you think you're pretty smart."

Jeanie looked the soldier up and down and replied, "You have no idea."

They continued chatting as they moved through the house. "What's in here?" Singer asked as he pointed to the hallway door on the main floor.

"Dad's home office. That's where he spends — I mean, *spent*, most of his time when he was home."

"Class 1 — main floor!" Singer yelled to his other team members. Class 1 was their designation for classified materials. This meant that what was inside had to be secured by one of the men while at least one other "mover" watched to confirm that the materials were packed with RFID chips, in special boxes and sealed with security tape; any tampering would be evident if the seal was later found to be broken. *RFID's* are *radio-frequency identification* tags which use electromagnetic fields to automatically identify and track the objects to which they are attached.

It also meant that these items had to be moved by a separate, more secure truck, so Sgt. Singer picked up his secure radio. "Dispatch. United One."

"Go ahead, United One," was the reply heard back in a woman's voice.

"United One is requesting a Turtle Box."

"Ten-four, United One. 20 is 1500 hours," which is military time for 3:00pm.

"Roger that," Sergeant Singer replied.

Promptly at 3:00pm., a smaller moving van arrived. Jeanie noticed that this was really more of an armored car than a moving van. The van was painted white with a logo of the moving company on each side. As she walked around the vehicle, she noted that the van had solid rubber tires, a steel-reinforced box and bullet-proof glass. She even noticed a sly little slot for a machine gun.

Sergeant Singer grabbed his radio one last time. "Dispatch. Turtle Box on station."

"Roger that," a voice cackled back. Now that the van for transporting the classified material was on the premises, Singer and the rest of the movers could finish packing the house. The three men meticulously tagged, cataloged and loaded the items that were located in Steve's office.

As they finished up, Jeanie walked through what she had called *home*...until today.

It's a strange feeling, she thought. *I have spent so much time trying to get away from here, and now that we're leaving, all I want to do is stay.* She looked at the empty room that used to be hers one last time, turned, and wandered outside.

Before long, the whole house had been loaded up. Sarah and Steve held hands as they took one last walk through the now-empty house where they spent the last fourteen years.

As the movers finished loading the van, Sarah took a deep breath and looked at Steve. "Okay, let's go," was all she could say as the images of their life in this house flashed in her head.

He reached down, took her hand and snuggled in close to her. "The adventure continues," he whispered in her ear.

She laid her head on his shoulder. "You know how I like a good adventure," she whispered back.

CHAPTER 3

A NEW START

While Steve stayed behind for a couple of days to wrap things up in the office, Sarah, Jeanie, and her little brother Mikey decided to begin the drive from Washington, DC. to their new home in Lakewood, Colorado. They all spent the night at a nearby Holiday Inn before going their separate ways first thing the following morning.

The next day, the sun was shining and there was not a cloud as far as the eye could see. Jeanie sat in the third-row back seat of a large black SUV. The sun was beating down on her face as she tried to imagine what her new life would be like, and she hoped that she would be able to make friends with kids her own age.

However, her active thoughts didn't help to pass the time; the drive seemed to take *forever*. The anticipation of the unknown and nervous excitement made time slow to a crawl. Even stops for food and bathroom visits did little to break up the dull roar of the tires on the interstate.

The drive through the plain states was extremely boring. There were miles and miles of farmland with very few towns or interstate exits. Her mother tried to help pass the time with idle chit-chat, but there was really nothing that would get through Jeanie's own thoughts. Not even her little brother's screaming, whining, and constant nonsense questions would attract her attention.

But there were ... *mountains*. As they started their ascent through the Rockies, Jeanie found herself gasping for breath as she cast her eyes upon the majestic landscape for the very first time. The peaks seemed to reach the heavens as the tertiary colors of the sunset settled on the mountaintops.

Oh...so beautiful, Jeanie thought. It was almost dusk, and the oranges, purples and pinks that crept onto the horizon seemed to be painted by the mountains themselves. Her brain seemed to hit *pause,* and all she could do was whisper to herself, *"Wow."* She was free from thinking about the move, the problems of being a kid genius, or what a new life in a new house in a new neighborhood might be like.

She had seen the mountains in pictures, but, as often happens, they could not compare to the real thing. This immense beauty helped Jeanie view her problems with a different perspective on a broader universe.

As in typical fashion, Jeanie's thoughts moved from the beauty of the mountains and sky to the vastness of the known universe. *In the grand scheme of things, it is easy to forget just how insignificant we are on this one small planet in our galaxy and within the universe as a whole.* Then she thought, *Even as a scientist, how could anyone believe that the creation of everything was just chance? It may not be politically correct, but the Big Bang Theory, which is thought to have created the universe and everything in it, I mean, it* has *to have been created by* something, *right?* These thoughts again helped Jeanie put her fears in perspective, and she relaxed just a little bit more.

After many hours on the road, Jeanie and Mikey were exhausted. Sarah decided it was time to call it a night, and really, she was ready for a break from driving.

Unlike Jeanie, who spent her time looking forward to a new life, Sarah spent most of the trip looking back on the one she had just left behind. She had become emotionally attached to their home, and she would miss the friends she'd made along the way. She was mad she didn't have a say in the move, the new house, or any of these huge and sudden decisions; however, her love for and support of her husband helped her find strength and comfort as she moved her family halfway across the country.

It was getting late, so Sarah pulled in front of a hotel, leaned over to Jeanie and whispered, "Stay in the car with your brother. I'm going in to register."

"Okay," said Jeanie with a sigh. She was tired of being cooped up but knew there was no point in arguing. She watched from the car as her mother pulled her driver's license and credit card from her purse, filled out a form and paid the desk clerk, and ten minutes later they were all getting settled into their hotel room.

The room was nothing special. There were two double beds, a small desk, a tiny fridge and a bathroom with a shower. Luckily, Jeanie would get one bed to herself, because her brother

Mikey slept like a *wiggle worm*, flip-flopping all night long, over and over again.

Sarah poked her head out through the window curtains to see the view. They were on the fifth floor, but it was dark with not too much to see. She pointed to the local diner across the street and said, "Who's hungry?"

Jeanie and Mikey both raised their hands and screamed "ME!" Mikey grabbed his mother's hand as they all walked out the door and headed across the street from the hotel in search of a bite to eat. There wasn't much traffic, and Mikey's little legs struggled to keep up with his mother's long stride.

The diner didn't seem like anything special. It was small, kind of on the *dirty* side, and even though there were a few tables with customers, there were plenty of seats available. With a quick scan of the room, Sarah chose a booth along the wall.

Sarah ushered Mikey to the inside as she scooched in to try and contain him. He fought his tiredness by wiggling around. "Hey, Mr. Squirm Worm," Sarah said as Jeanie slid into the seat opposite her. Normally, she would just carry him back to the room, but he had been strapped in a highchair all day and she really needed him to burn off some of that energy.

"Mom?" said Jeanie. "I'm nervous about starting all over. I mean, I'm excited and nervous all at the same time."

Sarah grabbed her daughter's hand softly and nodded as she replied, "Me, too. We have a lot of unknowns, but I tell ya' what; we'll get through this adventure together." Jeanie smiled a thin smile, shook her head in an approving nod, then grabbed a menu from behind the napkin holder to find something for dinner.

The waitress was wearing a retro pink dress like from a 1950's diner. She strolled up to the table smacking on chewing gum with *Tracy* embroidered on her chest. She looked at Jeanie and said, "What'd you like, hun?"

Jeanie really didn't like being called *hun*, and it kind of grossed her out to see the waitress smacking on her gum. "Ummm, can I just start with a Coke?"

Sarah pointed to Mikey and said, "Can he get a milk in a to-go cup, and I'll have water with lemon."

Tracy looked the family over while continuing to smack her gum and wrote down their drink orders. "I'll be right back to get your order." She then turned and walked back to the service counter.

They were all tired from the long ride and struggled to stay awake as the Smacker returned with their drinks. She placed a to-go cup with a lid filled with Coke in front of Jeanie and then passed out the rest of the beverages.

Sarah could see that Jeanie was close to the end of her rope, looked up to the server and said,

"Tracy, would you mind bringing her a *regular* cup? She's a little old for a sippy cup."

"Oh...sure thing," said the Smacker. "Lemme get your order, and I'll bring it right back."

That little gesture went a long way with Jeanie as she looked at her mom with a generally happy look of approval. She looked back over the menu and said, "Umm, can I get a plain cheeseburger and fries?"

Sarah pointed to the menu and said, "He'll take the kids' chicken tenders and I'll have just a salad." As Tracy left, Jeanie lifted her head and said, "Thanks, Mom." Sarah nodded, and the rest of the dinner was uneventful as they sat in silence and finished dinner. Afterwards, they returned to the hotel and fell fast asleep.

The next day, they all got up early and hit the road. Before Jeanie knew it, they were arriving at their new home. As they pulled in, Jeanie could see the movers had already arrived and begun unpacking. Then, as the GPS said, "You have reached your destination," she noticed two kids about her age, a boy and a girl, playing in the front yard of her new house.

She excitedly jumped out of the car even before her mother had finished pulling into the driveway. "Whoa! Wait for one more..." was all Jeanie's mom could get out before Jeanie leapt from the car. Bursting with excitement and energy after another long car ride, Jeanie ran into her new yard and introduced herself to the kids playing in front of her house.

"Hi, I'm ... I'm ... I'm Jeanie," she said breathlessly as she ran across the yard.

Not sure exactly how to react to the new-comer, who seems to be hyped up on Red Bull, the two kids looked at each other for a moment before the boy answered.

"Uh, hi. I'm Jimmy, but my friends call me Jimster. This is my sister Annie and we live next door." He pointed to the house to the right of

Jeanie's and motioned for her to follow him. Jeanie looked towards their house. It was a large two-story red brick house with two white columns in front, a large white pediment over the door, and tall skinny windows along the front of the house. It looked like it was a house that she would have found back in Virginia or D.C. She looked back towards her mom to make sure it was okay. Sarah smiled and motioned for Jeanie to go on as she helped Mikey get out of the back seat of the SUV.

The two kids had heard that someone was moving in next door, but the house had been empty for more than a year, so they often played in the yard. They didn't normally invite strangers to their house, but they wanted to be good neighbors, and Jeanie looked innocent enough.

Jimmy and Annie Jones were twelve-year-old twins, and they attended Lakewood Middle School, just three blocks from their house. Jimmy was a little taller than his sister; he had an athletic build for a twelve-year-old, brown hair and wore glasses. Annie was big for a twelve-year-old, with brown hair and brown eyes.

"I'm the smart one," she said, looking at Jeanie as she jabbed her brother with her elbow.

"Hey!" Jimmy shouted, as he was a little embarrassed by his sister's statement. Jeanie just nodded with a thin grin, not wanting to give away her secret and scare off her potential new friends.

"Where are you from?" Annie asked.

"We're from Baltimore, Maryland just outside of Washington, D.C." replied Jeanie.

"Wow! That's pretty cool," said Jimmy. "Have you been to the White House?"

"Yeah, I've been to the White House a couple of times," answered Jeanie. "I've even met the President. My parents didn't vote for him, but it was still cool to meet the *most powerful man in the world.*

"What do your parents do?" asked Annie.

"My mom, well...she is a stay-at-home mom. But she used to be a physicist before I was born. My dad is an engineer. His company moved us here because they needed him to head up some new project." Jeanie knew what the project was, but it was classified, and she couldn't tell her new companions. "How about you?"

"We're twins," said Annie, "and our family owns a restaurant not far from here."

"Do you get to eat for free?"

Annie said, "Yep! We usually go there after school."

"That's pretty cool. Do you get tired of eating off the same menu all of the time?" wondered Jeanie.

The twins looked at each other and shook their heads up and down, and said, "YES!" in unison. Everyone stopped and had a little laugh as the twins went to show Jeanie their bedrooms.

While Jeanie set off to make new friends, Sarah went to see their new house for the first time. "Steve was right; this house is *big*," she whispered to herself as she twisted the key in the lock to make sure it worked.

The house looked impressive from the street. The traditional Federalist-style home was 4,200 square feet, two stories with four bedrooms and a fully finished basement. The kitchen was large and equipped with a double Dutch oven and granite countertops. It had a large island in the middle that included an area large enough to accommodate four barstools.

The downstairs was painted a dark tan and had oak hardwood floors with white trim. Sarah walked through her new home, impressed with the overall size and feel as she said to herself, "Honey, I'm home," halfway expecting Steve to yell, "I'm in my office."

CHAPTER 4

FRIENDS!

J eanie, Jimmy and Annie became fast
friends, and Jeanie was elated to finally
have friends her own age. For now, it was pretty
easy to keep her secret because they were out
on summer break. Still, she couldn't help but
wonder how her new friends would react once
they discovered how freakishly smart she was.

*Would Jimmy and Annie think it's awesome
to have a genius as a friend,* Jeanie thought to
herself, *or would they be threatened like all of
the teachers and students from my old school?
Since they got to know me before they found*

out how smart I was, surely they would think of me as their neighbor and friend. But what if...?

After a couple of days had passed, Jeanie heard the familiar strum of her phone's ringtone. As she picked up, she heard Annie say, "Hey Jeanie! We are out running some errands and Mom is going to drop us off at the mall. Do you want to meet us?"

"Hold on," Jeanie replied excitedly. "Let me ask my mom." Annie could hear the echoes of Jeanie running through the house. Sarah was burnt out from unpacking. Jeanie ran up to her breathlessly and asked, "Mom, can you drop me at the mall so I can meet up with the twins?"

Sarah looked down at Jeanie's sweet face. "I guess so. A trip to the Colorado Mills Mall seems like a good idea. We need some groceries to fill this huge pantry anyway."

Jeanie held her phone to her ear and yelled, "SHE SAID 'YES!'"

Sarah loaded Mikey into his car seat and the three of them headed towards the interstate. It was only about a fifteen-minute drive to the mall. They had passed by a couple of times since they had arrived in Lakewood, but they had not yet ventured inside.

Sarah pulled into the mall parking lot and dropped Jeanie off between the Sports Authority and the Lakeview Police Department, which had a precinct in the mall. As Jeanie jumped out of the car, Sarah looked back and said, "Okay, honey, be careful."

Jeanie looked back and blew a kiss to her mother and yelled, "I will. Later!"

"Hey!" Sarah shouted out the window. "Call me when you're ready for me to pick you up."

"I will, but I might just ride home with the twins."

"Okay, sweetie. Just let me know." Then Sarah headed off to the grocery store.

As her mom drove off, Jeanie reached for her cell phone to text Jimmy and let him know that she was at the mall. "Here! Next to the police station."

As it happened, the twins were by the Super Target on the exact opposite side of the mall. It only took a few seconds before Jeanie's iPhone buzzed; she had a new text. The message read, "Wrong side. Take srvc hall to Trgt."

Looking up from her phone, she scanned the mall and quickly located the doors for the service hall that were just to her right. Jeanie hit the doors hard as she pushed her way into the hallway. She texted back, "OTW." *("On the way.")*

The service hall was very different than the rest of the mall. The walls were not painted and still showed signs of construction. It was dimly lit and a little spooky compared to the main mall area. Jeanie walked briskly but cautiously through the hall. As she approached the halfway point, she heard two men in a serious conversation coming towards her from a connecting hallway.

She stopped dead in her tracks. Oh no! Oh no! *I don't want to get in trouble for being in the service area. Mom will be mad if the police call her to come get me.* The entire length of the hall had doorways that were cut in about three feet from the main hall. She weighed her options and quickly ducked into one that was just to her right.

The cubby she dashed into was about four feet wide and had a red door along the back wall with a small sign that read, *Sunglass Hut.* She huddled in the corner that was closer to the men so she wouldn't be seen with a casual glance.

The men were in an intense conversation and paid little attention to the rest of their surroundings. They had accents, but she could not place the origin. Jeanie figured that they would probably pass by without even noticing she was there.

"How big does the device need to be?" the taller man asked. "I want to make sure it causes a total disruption to the system."

The other man waited a second or two before answering. "The effect will be plenty big. I promise you will be pleased with the result. Millions will be thrown back into the Stone Age. No power, no Internet, no nothing."

Jeanie's brain started to spin. *Millions without power? No nothing? Total devastation? What could...?*

As the thought came to her, she broke out in a cold sweat and her mouth dropped wide open. "Oh, no!" she whispered to herself. The physics of the device were swirling in her head.

As she watched them exit the service hall, she knew they were talking about the U.S. Power Grid. Only a nuclear blast or an EMP (Electromagnetic Pulse) could cause the kind of devastation they were describing. Such a device would disable the brains of the new *Smart Power Grid*.

The *Smart Power Grid* is a computer-controlled network of electric companies and power plants. It is used to quickly and efficiently route power throughout the country to where it is needed most. The United States government has done a pretty good job of modernizing its power grid, but it could be very susceptible to this kind of attack. Jeanie knew that an EMP detonation, either in the air or on the ground near one of the power grid control centers, could move the country into chaos.

How did they put it? *Into the Stone Age,* they said.

She stayed silently huddled in the corner as her cubby seemed to shrink around her, but she sat still until she knew the two had exited the passage. She thought to herself...

Man One: tall, well-dressed in expensive clothing, dark hair, glasses, carrying a leather computer-type bag.

Man Two: shorter, around 5' 10", dirty shoes, jeans and a Broncos ball cap.

Once she had a mental picture of the two men, Jeanie whispered to herself, "Holy CRAP!" She couldn't believe what she had just heard. She nervously began to decipher the plans she had just intercepted.

Jeanie knew that there would only be a few ways to create a magnetic pulse large enough to disable a system that covered such a large area. One way would be with a nuclear device; the other would require the use of several large condensers connected together with a major power source and a large copper coil.

She also knew that a large-scale disruption of the *Smart Grid* would have disastrous results to life in the United States and parts of Canada. This system took many years to get up and running and it would be difficult and very expensive to repair.

After another minute, she took off running through the hall toward the Super Target where Jimmy and Annie watched as their friend came bursting through the doors from the hall.

Jeanie was as white as a ghost. "Jeanie? You okay?" Annie asked.

"You guys are not going to believe what just happened," she replied shakily and halfway out of breath.

The Jones twins did not know Jeanie's secret about being some kind of super genius, but they soon would. Even though Jeanie would have liked to keep her secret longer, she felt that this bit of information would be crucial in her efforts to convince Jimmy and Annie to help her stop these men from destroying the country.

Jeanie pulled her friends to a quiet corner. She wanted to make sure that as few people could hear her as possible. "You guys aren't going to believe what just happened," she started. "I was walking through the hall and I heard two men coming towards me from the adjoining hall. I hid in one of the doorways and I heard them talk about planning a terror attack!"

Jimmy tilted his head and smirked. "Come on, Jeanie," he said in a sarcastic voice. Annie, however, could see how disturbed their new friend seemed to be and showed a little more interest in hearing Jeanie's story.

"Shut up, Jimmy!" she said. "Go ahead, Jeanie, tell us what happened," Annie urged.

"Okay," Jeanie said. "*Jeez, I'm shaking*...but before I do, there is something I need to tell you. I'm very smart. Well, not just very smart, but *very, very smart.*"

Jimmy snickered again and looked at his sister, amused with the story he was hearing. "Yeah, Jeanie, and I invented the Internet," he said. To be fair, the twins had not seen anything that would substantiate her claims.

Jeanie could understand why he didn't believe her, but she continued. "My IQ is close to 160, and the only reason I'm a senior in high school is because my parents weren't ready for me to go to college. I am considered one of the most intelligent people in the country and maybe the world. My areas of expertise are science, technology and applied mathematics and my memory is nearly perfect. Some people might call it a *photographic memory*. I would say it's more like an *Eidetic memory*. That basically means that I can remember all sorts of information and not just images of memories used for recall."

"Hold on, Jeanie ... you're a senior in *high school?*" Jimmy asked sarcastically.

"Yes."

"Most intelligent in the world? Come on!" He continued his line of questioning.

"I know it is hard to believe, and you two don't know me that well, but it is true...I swear!"

Annie, seeing how upset Jeanie was, looked to her brother and said, "Come on, Jimmy, let's hear her out. I believe her."

"Okay, I'll hear her out."

Jimmy and Annie listened as Jeanie went into detail about her parents and her relationship with NGT. She reached into her purse and pulled out her ID card that showed her photo along with her name and the title freelance *consultant* listed below.

The more she spoke, the more the twins believed her story. "Whoa, that's so cool," Jimmy mumbled as she finished her story. The twins just looked at each other with wide eyes.

Then Jeanie said, "You have to come with me to the police station!" She remembered it was located where she entered the mall. Jimmy and Annie were hesitant, but they believed Jeanie's story.

"I don't know. The police?" Annie said.

"They won't believe us. We're just kids," Jimmy added.

Jeanie grabbed Annie by the wrist. "Come on!" she said, leading her friends back toward the police station.

The three ran back through the service hall that had started this whole adventure. Jeanie stopped just outside the station to catch her breath and regain her composure.

Even though her heart was pumping hard, Jeanie calmly walked into the Lakeview Police station. She walked up to the desk sergeant and said, "I need to speak to a detective right away."

The sergeant behind the counter took one look at Jeanie and her two friends and asked her, "What's this about?"

"I need to report a terror attack."

"Really, a terror attack? Where?" The officer smirked.

"I don't know where. I just know it's going to happen," said Jeanie.

"Really? And how do you know that?"

"I heard two men talking about it in the service hall."

"And when is this attack supposed to take place?"

"I don't know! Don't be so obtuse!" She yelled at the desk sergeant.

Jimmy and Annie could tell the officer was getting annoyed, and it didn't seem like Jeanie calling him names was going to help.

Annie grabbed Jeanie by the arm. "We'd better go."

"No! We need to see a detective!" insisted Jeanie.

"Go home or I'll will call your parents," said the officer.

"Look," Jeanie insisted once more. "I have information about a terror attack!" Jeanie's voice was starting to get a little louder and she was clearly agitated by the desk sergeant. Jimmy and Annie were terrified. They tried to pull Jeanie way, but she wriggled free and said, "Listen, I just told you I had information about a terror attack. I need to speak to a detective right now!"

The sergeant was clearly not amused. "Kid, what is your number?" Jeanie reluctantly gave him her dad's cell number. She figured that he would look at the caller ID and just not pick up.

She was wrong. Steve was just pulling into Lakewood when his phone rang. The caller ID read *Lakeview Police Dept.* He quickly grabbed the phone. "Hello?"

"Mr. Miller. This is Sgt. Jackson with the Lakeview Police Department. Your daughter Jeanie is here claiming to have information about a terror attack."

Fifteen minutes later, he arrived at the mall and entered the police station. He walked up to the desk and said, "I'm here to see Sergeant Jackson." The desk officer pointed to a desk in the back of the office where Steve saw Jeanie and her friends. He walked back to the desk and looked down at his daughter and her friends and said to the officer, "A terror attack? Really?"

He glanced over to the twins who would not make eye contact as Jimmy kind of shrugged his shoulders. "Uh-huh."

Jeanie's dad was visibly upset. Her overactive imagination had never resulted in a phone call from the police before. They had just arrived in Lakewood, and the last thing Steve needed was to call attention to himself and his family. He loved Jeanie, but he could not understand why she needed to pretend so much. He truly appreciated her intellect but sometimes he wished she could be more like a normal kid.

Jeanie looked up with glossy eyes. "Dad, I swear I know..." He cut her off by putting his finger to his lips. "Shhh. We'll discuss this later. Let's go."

Jeanie understood what he meant.

All three kids slid into the black leather seats in the back of the SUV. The twins just kind of looked at each other, not really knowing what to do, and they were embarrassed to meet Jeanie's dad this way. Jimmy leaned over to Annie and whispered real low, "What are we going to tell Mom and Dad?"

Annie just looked back and shrugged. It was quiet in the car the rest of the ride home. Jeanie just looked straight ahead with a blank stare on her face, which made the twins even more nervous. They wondered about Jeanie and were worried about what they didn't know about her past.

As Steve was pulling off the highway, he reached for his phone and called Sarah to relay the events of the evening. The three kids sat in back just looking at each other, not sure what to do next. Jeanie, however, knew what she had heard was real, and she was determined to stop the bad guys, whether her dad believed her or not.

When she got home, she ran to her room and slammed the door. Steve and Sarah just looked at each other as Sarah motioned with her right hand low as if she were pushing something to the ground. Steve understood that this meant to let her go.

"We'll talk to her later," said Sarah, as she started to get dinner ready.

Chapter 5

HUNTING FOR TERRORISTS

J eanie sat up in her bed all night thinking about the day's events. She looked on her phone for as much information she could find searching *EMPs* and the *Smart Electric Grid*.

It was a long night, and Jeanie watched the sun come up over the horizon. She went downstairs, ate some breakfast, and waited for her friends to wake up.

Around 9:00am, Jeanie walked next door to talk with the twins. Annie and her brother were sitting on the couch eating cereal and watching something on Netflix when they heard the knocks at the door. Annie could see through the window it was Jeanie. "I'll get it," Annie said to her brother as she got up to answer the door.

Still upset from yesterday, she cracked the door open and said, "Yes?"

"Can I come in?" asked Jeanie. "I feel horrible that yesterday ended the way it did."

"You should!" Jimmy yelled from the couch. "We got in trouble, too."

"I know. I'm sorry. I don't want this incident to put a strain on our friendship. Can I come in?"

"Yeah, sure," Annie said as she opened the door all the way to let her in.

"I want you to know that I'm not crazy, and I'm not making this up," Jeanie said. "I heard what I heard. I think we can do something, but I need your help."

Jeanie started by relaying all of the information she had found about EMPs and the Smart Grid. Then she went on to describe every little detail about the two men and their conversation.

This was a lot for the twins to take in, but ultimately, Jeanie was so convincing and had so much detail the two assumed that she was telling the truth because *who would make up a story like that?*

When Jeanie was done, the three just sat in silence for a few minutes as the information sunk in. "So, what now?" Jimmy uttered. Together, the three brainstormed as to how to stop the terrorists from destroying life as they knew it in the United States.

"Well...we know we can't go to the authorities," Jimmy said.

"Nope," Jeanie replied. "We tried that last night and took the ride of shame home from the police station."

"What about the FBI (Federal Bureau of Investigation)?" Annie asked.

"I just don't think they'll believe three kids. Even with my credentials and my clearance status."

They sat there looking at each other for what seemed like hours. Jeanie tried to analyze their situation from every angle and still could not decide what the best course of action might be.

Jimmy said, "What if we sent an anonymous tip to Homeland Security?"

"Good thought," Jeanie said, "but by the time they got around to investigating, if they ever did, it could likely be too late. I think we'll need a course of action that triggers an immediate investigation. That is our best chance of stopping the attack."

Then suddenly Annie yelled, "Since the authorities won't believe us, why don't we hire our own spies to track down the bad guys?"

Jeanie and Jimmy looked at each other for a second. Then a light bulb went off in Jeanie's head. "Yeah, why not?" she said in a soft voice.

"But how?" Jimmy asked.

The three thought for another minute, then Jeanie said, *"Craigslist!"*

Craigslist is an online clearinghouse for just about everything. There is a local portal in every major city, and you can post things for sale, things that you are looking to buy and classified ads for all types of goods and services.

Jeanie thought this would be an ideal way to post and track interest ... with an ad.

Surging with excitement, Jeanie, Jimmy and Annie ran back over to Jeanie's house, up the stairs and straight into her room. Once again, the door slammed.

"What should we do first?" Annie asked.

"I feel like we should try to stay as anonymous as possible," said Jeanie. "Let's create a new Gmail account first, then we can setup the Craigslist ad."

"That's smart," Jimmy added.

Jeanie looked over her left shoulder to where Jimmy was sitting and said, "Well, you know." Her little joke brought a light-hearted chuckle from the room.

They gathered around Jeanie's desk as she hopped onto her MacBook Air. She quickly navigated the keys to get past her login screen, then pulled up a web browser. With a smile on her face, Jeanie completed the setup for the new Gmail account.

"Now that that's done, we can go ahead and submit our ad," said Jeanie. She logged into Craigslist under a fake name. Her ad read simply, "Spies Wanted." An automated generic Craigslist reply email went immediately to the new Gmail account that Jeanie had set up.

"Now what?" Annie asked.

"Now we wait and see what happens," Jeanie replied.

The rest of the day, the three walked through the neighborhood. They wandered from place to place, talking about their mission and wondering if and when their ad on Craigslist might generate some interest.

It wasn't long before the inbox of their new account was full of inquiries. The three friends read through each email that they received and deleted several that were *obviously* not from *real* spies. They really hadn't known what to expect, and they spent what seemed like hours going through all of the email that they received.

Chapter 6

BUILDING A TEAM

―――――――――

This was a strange time for the clandestine spy agencies in the United States. For over seventy years, the United States had relied on its intelligence gathering to protect the American people. The National Security Agency (NSA) and the Central Intelligence Agency (CIA) together had been largely responsible for the information about weapons of mass destruction (WMDs) that had led to the Gulf War following the terrorist attacks in New York City on September 11, 2001.

Currently, however, national politics had forced the downsizing of the two agencies responsible for our foreign intel. A political shift and the slow economy were the main issues, causing Congress to shrink the budgets of these agencies. This is why retired and newly released agents were now seeking new employment.

"To be honest, I really didn't think our plan would work," Jimmy said. He was amazed to see that they had received many replies. Most of the responses were automated ads, spam, or questions about part-time work from what were clearly other kids. Others, however, the ones they considered to be real possibilities, were short replies like, *"Contact name - Brock 305-555-5555."* Annie was responsible for writing down the contact names and phone numbers for those that looked most promising.

"How do we call them back?" Jimmy asked.

"We need to get a throw-away phone," Jeanie said.

Annie looked at her and replied, "What's that?"

"You know how, when you go into a 7-Eleven or a grocery store, and they have a display with cell phones for sale? You know? You buy the phone and then you buy a card with minutes on it to activate the phone," Jeanie said. "We can buy one of those and the number will be nearly impossible to track. I mean, they won't be secure or encrypted or anything like that, but it will be hard to track it back to us," she continued.

"Smart," Jimmy said again with a smile on his face.

Annie punched him in the arm and said, "Duh."

Again, the three laughed. Jeanie was happy that her friends didn't see her intellect as a total turnoff. For so long, she had been made fun of and bullied because of her IQ. It was refreshing to have true friends who accepted her as she was.

Excited by their success, the three friends took their list of names, hopped on their bikes and rode to the convenience store that was only a couple of blocks away. Jeanie took out her check card and took $100 from the ATM. *Better to pay in cash; a credit card charge might lead back to the phone*, she thought. She picked out an inexpensive smartphone and grabbed a pre-paid card with 120 minutes of talk time on it.

They anxiously paid for their things and hurriedly ran out to the parking lot. Jimmy ripped open the phone packaging while Jeanie gave him the activation card and said, "We need to find a public computer in order to activate the phone. We don't want to leave any traces back to where we purchased the *drop phone*; that's what they call 'em."

"Dang!" Jimmy said.

The twins looked back to each other as if they had a telepathic connection. They said in unison, "The library!"

Everyone jumped on their bikes and pedaled as fast as they could to the public library. They skidded up to the front of the building, dropped their bikes in the grass, and shot for the entrance. The automatic doors opened as they approached, and the three ran through, making *way* too much noise.

The librarian at the front counter was quite young; she looked to be in her twenties and a little like an overstuffed teddy bear, with short black hair with purple ends. She glanced over her retro horn-rimmed glasses, put her finger over her mouth and made a loud *"SHHHHHH!"*

Immediately the three stopped running but continued to the computer area with a fast walk. The librarian watched them for a few more seconds, then went back to checking books back in from the return bin.

The computer was new by library standards - a Dell desktop PC, probable two years old, running Windows. It ran fine, and it took Jeanie only a couple of minutes to get logged in under a fake name.

"Now that we're in, all I need to do is enter the fake information we created from the Gmail account," relayed Jeanie to the twins.

"Then what?" Jimmy asked.

"Well ... once we have entered all the info from the phone, we should be able to use the new phone number to contact our prospects," she answered.

"So cool," Annie chimed in.

Once she entered all of the required information, the phone was up and running. Jeanie looked at the team and gave them a thumbs-up. "We're good to go," she told them. "Jimmy, why don't you go up to the librarian and ask if you can use the phone. Then dial this number so we can make sure it works before we leave."

Jimmy went back to the librarian and asked, "Can I please use the phone to call my mom to come get us? My bike is broken." Without even looking up, she handed him the desk phone and continued checking in books. He called the number for their new drop phone, and it immediately rang. Jeanie didn't answer but Jimmy stayed at the desk phone for another thirty seconds, then hung up and handed the phone back to the librarian. "Thanks. She didn't answer."

Now that they knew the phone was activated, the team could start calling each number that Annie had written down and make arrangements to meet the prospective spies at the mall food court.

First though, Jeanie wanted to see what information she could find, if any, about the potential applicants. "Hey guys, I want to log in to the system to see if there is any information about our applicants before we start making calls."

"Great idea," Jimmy answered, "but how?"

"When we get back to my house, I'll use Dad's security login to see if there is anything in the CIA's or Interpol's databases."

"What's Interpol?" Annie asked.

"Oh ... sorry," Jeanie answered. "*Interpol* is an international police organization that basically keeps track of international criminals."

"Yeah, we definitely need to do ... whatever that is that you just said," said Annie.

"I also think we need our own code names," suggested Jeanie as they sat on the ground outside the library.

Jimmy loved the idea and immediately yelled, "'Rocker!' I'll be 'Rocker.'" He was a pretty good guitar player and dreamed about playing in a rock 'n' roll band, so *Rocker* was the first thing that popped into his head. After he said it, he stopped and wondered if that really was the name he wanted; ultimately he decided that it was a cool name.

Annie said, "'Peanut.' I wanna be 'Peanut.'" Rocker snickered and looked at his sister with a funny face.

"Why Peanut?" Jeanie asked.

"It's my hamster's name, and I always liked that name," answered Annie. They all started to laugh. "What's wrong with that?" She did like that name.

You could tell that Jeanie was thinking hard about what she wanted her name to be. She sat with her head resting on her hand as she looked up to the right, trying to recall all of the great women of history and mythology.

"Well?" Annie asked.

"Hold on. I'm … " Finally she said, "I'll be 'Athena.'" She thought that there would be no better name to describe her.

"Why Athena? I mean, what's so great about Athena?" Rocker asked.

Jeanie answered, "Athena was born of Zeus, who was basically, like, the king of the gods. She wasn't born like anyone else; she just sprang from Zeus's head, fully grown. She was a brave and fierce fighter," she told her friends. "She only went to war to defend her home from outside enemies. She was also known as the goddess of wisdom, courage, law and justice, strategic warfare, mathematics, strategy and a bunch of other things." Jeanie thought to herself, *I am Athena!*

"Oh...I love that name," Annie said. "That is so cool." The three sat together, impressed with their new identities and ready to carry out the rest of their mission.

"Now what?" Rocker asked.

"Okay, gang. Here's what I think we should do," Athena said to her crew. "Once we background check everybody, let's have each applicant sit at a specific table in the mall food court. On each table we can leave a packet of information that includes a brief about the threat, our new contact information including the drop phone number, and our code names. Let's go back to my house and I'll type up and print out instructions."

The three hopped on their bikes, rode back to Athena's house as fast as they could and headed up to her room. She swirled her chair around, sat down, and spun herself to face her computer. Rocker and Peanut peered over her shoulder, one on each side.

It only took Athena a few minutes to type up the information for each applicant. Each potential spy was instructed to call the number of the drop phone and leave their own code name, phone number, and email address ... along with their required compensation for the mission. Jeanie then went down to her father's office and plugged in whatever information the trio had received from the Craigslist ads, but it was just too vague to give any meaningful response.

The food court meetings were set for the next day at 1:00pm. It didn't take long until they had confirmation from each of the spies they had contacted through Craigslist. "Now we just have to wait," Athena said aloud as she wondered if any of their prospects knew each other from previous jobs.

"I'm on pins and needles," Rocker chimed in.

"What are we going to do now? If we just sit here, I'm gonna to go crazy with nervous excitement," Peanut added.

"I know … right?" Athena answered. "Let's review all of the details one more time …"

1. Coordinate with our parents to get to the mall.

2. Print out all of the packets and stuff them in envelopes.

3. Place packets at specific tables.

"Okay, got it," Peanut answered. "I'll check with our mom to see if she'll take us to the mall tomorrow. Rocker, why don't you help Athena put the packets together?"

"Ten-four," Rocker replied. "When you're done with mom, meet us back here and we'll finish up,"

Jeanie giggled, "We should say 'roger' or 'roger that.' It's what they say in the military." Peanut smiled, gave them a thumbs-up and headed off to ask her mom to take them to the mall on the following day.

The next day, they arrived at the mall early, placed the packets at the assigned tables, then walked around the mall anxiously awaiting the arrival of the spies. "Don't worry guys. We got this," Athena said to her crew.

The plan went flawlessly. The applicants all arrived on time at their respective tables. Athena, Peanut, and Rocker were able to get photos of each individuals with their iPhones as they, one-by-one, picked up their packets. Not one of the spies could have ever imagined that it was a bunch of kids needing their help, so the kids were able to hide in plain sight.

It wasn't long before they had phone messages from each of the applicants. The three listened to each of the messages as Peanut wrote down their code names, email addresses, phone numbers and salary requests.

"Holy cow! I can't believe that actually worked," Peanut mused out loud.

"I know, right?" Rocker chimed in.

"Well, gang, it looks like we're in business," Athena added. And with that, their new spy agency was up and running. "Can you believe we have our very own team of international spies?"

The friends were impressed with themselves and by what they had accomplished. "I think this deserves a cookie break," said Rocker.

"I think you're right. We *do* deserve a cookie break," his sister answered, big grin stretching across her face.

"Yes, I agree," stated Jeanie matter-of-factly. "I think cookies should be a fitting treat after launching our own international spy agency."

Rocker and Peanut looked at each other and laughed at Athena's reply. "You're such a geek,"

Rocker added. "Now let's go get some dang cookies already!"

With the completion of their cookie break, it was time to get back to business. They reviewed all of the applications and agreed on three applicants.

First, there was a man with the code name "Brock." Brock was of average height and build. He stood about five foot, ten inches tall. In his photo, he had a thick blonde mustache and hair and wore dark sunglasses and a New York Yankees ball cap. Jeanie was sure that the mustache was fake, but she was impressed by his ability to change his appearance.

According to his resume, Brock was a former Navy Seal who spent three years working in Ukraine with the NSA (National Security Agency), where he spent time both as a field agent and Deputy Station Chief before he retired from the agency. Because of his age and experience, Athena thought Brock could be the leader of the group.

Next came "Roxy." Roxy was a beautiful brunette in her mid-thirties. She had a slender build and stood about five-six. In her photo, she was well dressed, wearing a navy pinstripe business suit with a knee-length skirt. She was ex-military intelligence and honorably discharged a little more than a year earlier. She spent most of her military time in Germany running Psychological Operations (Psy-Ops) against al-Qaeda groups within Europe. Because of her background, Roxy would be in charge of communications for the group.

Then there was "Jonah," a twenty-five-year-old ex-Green Beret. He was in excellent shape with a slender but muscular frame. He joined the military straight out of high school and was recruited by the CIA when he was twenty. He had just completed his training before he was sidelined by budget cuts. Jonah would be the *tracker*; his primary function would be to chase down leads in the field while the others worked electronic intel.

"Now we need to get the three together and start *Operation Liberty Torch*," Athena said in a whisper, not wanting to draw any extra attention. She loved her country and enjoyed working with her father on projects that ultimately helped to keep the country safe. The twins liked the mission name, but Peanut wondered if it had a deeper meaning as so many things with Athena did.

"What does it mean?" Peanut leaned in to ask Athena.

"Well," explained Athena, "the Statue of Liberty, or 'Lady Liberty,' was given to the United States as a symbol of freedom and friendship from the French. She carries the Liberty Torch. It was dedicated in 1866. I felt that it represents our friendship and our desire to protect the freedoms our Constitution provides."

The three stood and had a group hug. "That's so cool," said Rocker as he gave his sister and Athena each a big bear hug.

CHAPTER 7

THE SPY GAME

When the time came to get the new spy team together the following day, Athena reached for the drop phone the team had purchased from the convenience store. *Safer to remain anonymous,* she figured. She had even installed an app that would change her voice when calling their prospective spies. She wanted the voice to sound male, and with a few clicks, she had the phone ready to go. She read the message she had written out the previous night three times out loud as practice before making the calls.

The message was simple: "Tuesday, 3:00pm, Union Square Park, playground. Wear a Philadelphia Eagles ball cap."

Athena took the time to write out a complete account of the events from the last couple of nights, including dates, times and exact locations. She included schematics of the mall, the location of the police station and individual assignments for each of the new agents. Once she completed the dossiers, she ran downstairs from her room and asked, "Mom, can you take us to the to the park for the afternoon?"

Sarah looked at her watch and said, "Sure, I have time." She grabbed Mikey and loaded him in his car seat as Athena, Rocker and Peanut climbed into the back of the SUV.

Rocker fidgeted back and forth for the entire ride while Peanut continuously bounced her knee. Athena leaned her head against the window with a blank stare as they approached the park.

"Boy, you are awful quiet. What's going on?" asked Sarah. "I thought you guys would be all revved up since you were so eager to get to the park."

Rocker and Peanut just looked at each other with a surprised look. "We're just thinking," Athena answered. "We're planning a new game, a scavenger hunt, and we're just trying to figure out what we're going to get each other to hunt for."

Good save, Rocker thought to himself.

"Yeah, you know … we're thinking about stuff for the hunt." Peanut added.

"Oh, that sounds fun. Let me know how it goes!"

"Will do, Mom," responded Athena.

As Sarah pulled into the park, Athena perked up and said, "Thanks, Mom; can you just let us out here?"

"Here? You want me to let you out *here*?" asked her mother.

"Yeah. That would be great. We want to start the scavenger hunt here."

Sarah looked in her rearview mirror and pulled over to the side of the playground area. "Okay, well, give me a call when you're ready to come home!" Sarah yelled as the three grabbed their stuff and piled out of the back of the SUV.

They had arrived at the park about two hours before the stated time of the meeting. Athena expected their spies to show up early to recon the situation, and her team needed time to get ready in advance.

"Rocker," Athena said, "will you take the signs we made and place one on each end of the playground with the arrows pointing this way?" Athena motioned to where they were standing. Rocker lowered his ball cap and pushed his sunglasses further up on his face; he thought it made him look cooler. He posted a sign near each end of the playground that read, "Eagles Fan Club Meeting 3:00pm."

Athena left one of the completed mission dossier packets where she and Peanut were standing. Again, the dossier was in a white envelope with a printed label that read *Eagles Fan Club*. "Do you think it will be okay if we just leave the packet here?" Peanut asked.

Athena thought for a moment, smirked a little and shrugged her shoulders. "I'm not 100% sure," she said. "We'll need to sit over at the edge of the playground and act like we're playing some kind of game so we can keep an eye on the dossier."

Things went as planned. Rocker, Peanut, and Athena played it cool, pretending to play and watching from a distance as the members of this new spy agency arrived for their first meeting. One by one, the covert team showed up early, as expected, allowing time to recon the park before the scheduled rendezvous.

Brock pulled up first, driving a late-model Chevy Impala, black with black tinted windows.

It looked like an unmarked police car. He stepped out and started to look around the park.

While Brock was poking around, Jonah pulled into the park and stopped next to the black Chevy. He was driving a sporty silver Audi two-door. He got out of his car, grabbed a camera from the front seat, pulled his Eagles cap down low and started wandering around, taking pictures and surveying the scene.

Fifteen minutes later, Roxy pulled in, two spaces to the right of the black Impala. She wore dark blue skinny jeans, an Eagles T-shirt and ball cap. She had also brought a camera; hers had a telephoto lens and clearly produced better photos than her phone could. She set her iPhone to record her GPS location with one of her fitness apps, pulled out a digital audio recorder and slid it into her back pocket. It wasn't long before the three ran into each other.

"I guess we're all here for the 'fan club meeting,'" Roxy said. Both Brock and Jonah were taken aback by the beautiful woman standing in front of them.

Jonah puffed out his chest and stood a little taller as he held out his hand and introduced himself. "Jonah, nice to meet you," he said.

"I'm Roxy," she replied.

Brock moved in closer and stuck his hand out and said "Brock. Nice to meet you both." With the introductions over, Brock looked at his watch and said to the group, "Shall we go see why we're all here?"

The three cautiously followed the signs to the drop point, picked up the information packets, also known as a dossiers, and looked over the information that Athena and the crew had left for them. Each of the spies was on edge and moving with heightened awareness. None of them knew who was trying to hire their services, and they were each wary of one another, as they had never worked together in the past.

They walked as Brock read the dossier out loud for the newly assembled group. Once he completed the initial review of the documents that were provided by their unseen bosses, Roxy said, "I could hack the mall security system and download a copy of the security footage from that night. That should let us get a good look at the service hall and track the movements of the two suspects."

Brock looked up from the paper and acknowledged Roxy's mission. "Jonah, you contact the police department and see if there were any strange vehicles reported in the area; I'll beat the bushes to see if we can rattle cages," Brock said.

Once they completed their initial review, Roxy looked out from under the bill of her ball cap and said, "Do either of you know anything about *Mission Command?*" This is a term commonly used to identify those who are funding and running a particular operation or *ops*.

Both Jonah and Brock shook their heads. "Nope. Look, let us know what you see on the video. That may help us know something more about our mission," Brock said. Then with a brief nod the three headed back to their cars and were off, each in their own direction.

Athena, Peanut and Rocker kept their distance ... but business was underway.

Roxy was staying at a Hampton Suites a few blocks from the mall. After getting something to eat, she returned to her room and went straight to work. She reached for her suitcase and pulled out a laptop, an encrypted wireless broadband card and an electronic bug detector. Even though she knew chances were slim-to-none that she was being followed or bugged, it was a habit she had developed during her time in military intelligence.

After sweeping the room, she booted up her computer and connected to the Internet by using VPN (virtual private network) software. Roxy always used a VPN to connect to the Internet in order to mask her identity and location, just in case her network intrusions were ever detected. It didn't take long before she hacked the mall's firewall and found the video she was looking for in the security system. It only took her only a few minutes to get the files and disconnect from their network. This was a fairly easy task that she had learned as part of her U.S. intelligence training; her activities had rarely, if ever, been detected … even by the most sophisticated governments.

The mall had virtually every inch of the property covered by video cameras. She found where the two men had entered the hall and followed them out to the parking lot and into their cars. She grabbed their plate numbers and forwarded the information to Jonah. The only thing that seemed out of the ordinary was the young girl she noticed as the only other person in the hall, hiding in a doorway at the same time the suspected terrorists were passing through the service hall.

While Roxy was downloading the footage, Brock headed back to his hotel. He was staying at the Microtel. This low-budget motel had the room essentials, but few amenities and even less comfort. Brock could afford nicer hotels, but he liked the harder beds in the cheaper ones. He figured it was because of the time he spent on active duty as a soldier in Ukraine; that had been tough. Once he got out of the service, he had never really adjusted back to the comfortable lifestyle he had known before his time in the army.

Once in his room, he pulled his computer from his bag and plopped it on the desk. Brock used a rugged military-grade computer. It was heavy and bulky, but it could take a beating. He connected to his Wi-Fi card and launched his own VPN software in order to connect to the Internet. Like Roxy, Brock didn't want to leave fingerprints of his search. He was looking for unusual web chatter that might indicate terrorist activity in the United States.

Before, long he had discovered a disturbing trend. There was a lot of communications about a guy named "Palo V." He gathered all of the information he'd found and printed out each page. He'd give it all to Roxy once they reconnected to see if she could find any additional patterns in the data.

Jonah took the plate numbers that Roxy had given him and ran a trace in order to find names and addresses of the owners. The first plate belonged to a man named Frasier York, who showed to be living at 1231 Birdview Avenue, Malibu, CA. A quick Google search showed that Mr. York was a movie producer, who specialized in action films. The second plate lead to Hertz rental cars, at the airport. Jonah went there first.

It was a thirty-minute drive to the airport in normal traffic. Jonah was mulling over the details of the mission that he had so far to see if he could make other connections. When he arrived at the airport, he parked in short-term parking and headed to the car rental area; Hertz was loaded with customers.

Jonah had put on a well-tailored dark navy business suit, a white button-down shirt and a red tie. *Time to look the part,* he thought. He walked in with confidence and headed straight to the counter, flashed an ID and asked for the manager.

He kept several IDs depending on the situation. Today, he carried an FBI badge. The girl behind the counter gestured for Jonah to proceed to the office around the corner.

Sitting at the desk was a very attractive blonde wearing twill slacks and a navy blazer. Her nametag read *Natalie Singer*.

Jonah turned on the charm. He flashed his ID and asked her, "Can you tell me about a silver Mercedes E-Class that was rented from this location earlier in the week?" He handed the plate number over to her.

"Let's see," she said as she punched a few keys on the computer. "I should make you get a warrant for this info," she said while she printed out the information that was on her screen.

"Now why would you want to go and do a thing like that?" he replied, leaning onto her desk. She reached down to her printer, grabbed the sheet of paper from her printer, wrote something on it and handed it to Jonah. Jonah purposefully, but ever so lightly touched her hand as he accepted the paper from her delicate fingers.

He glanced at the paper and saw that Natalie had written *@nat_sing25 (865-555-5555)*. He looked back to her as he prepared to leave. "Give me a call sometime," she said.

"Roger that," he replied, and he winked at her as he headed out the door.

The name at the top of the page was Farhan Kholi. The printout also included a copy of Kholi's passport and his driver's license. While it wouldn't be that unusual for people from Bollywood to travel to Hollywood, it was a little strange that they would meet in the sub-urbs of Denver.

Jonah took the information from Hertz and left to meet Brock and Roxy at her hotel for dinner. Both were already sitting in the corner of the restaurant when he arrived, carrying a little extra swagger as he approached the table. He stood in front of his new teammates, reached into his pocket, and slammed the piece of paper he received from Hertz on the table.

Roxy reached over to examine the sheet. "What's this?" she asked, turning the paper around to reveal a woman's handwritten phone number.

"Whoa! Wrong one," Jonah said with a smirk and a wink at Roxy.

"Oh please," she shot back to him.

"All right, gang. Down to business," Brock broke in.

Jonah reached back into his pocket and pulled out the information that he had collected, laying it on the table. Roxy picked up the new sheet, looked it over and started punching keys on her computer. "This is more like it," she said as she retrieved information regarding Mr. Kholi's travel. "Okay, looks like our Mr. Kholi is supposed to be a movie director who is wanting to expand to the United States."

Brock had his own stack of printouts about an inch thick. "This is web chatter," he said. "Each one mentions Palo V." Brock was sure that something was going on, but he did not know what or how the two suspects fit into the scheme.

The three spies looked at each other for a minute without saying a word. "Roxy," Jonah said. "Isn't there a *power plant* in *Palo Verde*?"

Roxy turned her attention back to her laptop, then she turned it around for the others to see. "Yes. The Palo Verde Generating Station is a large nuclear power plant in Arizona; besides generating power for folks living in Arizona, it also supplies energy for a large section of Southern California."

"Surely this would be a high-value target. Roxy, what have *you* got?" Brock said.

"As you know, I hacked the security video from the mall. There was an odd thing on the video," Roxy said. She brought up the mall security footage and pointed to the girl huddled in the corner.

Brock looked up from the screen and glanced at both Roxy and Jonah and said, "Huh. What do you make of that? Well, we'll file that away for later. For now, let's follow up on these leads."

Still, Brock couldn't help but think to himself, *Could it be? We've already been paid. Money was transferred to their offshore accounts — some things just aren't adding up.*

The group pondered what all they'd discovered and their current situation and decided to check further into the girl on the video - to see where she might fit in.

Chapter 8

SEARCHING FOR A TERRORIST

Brock took all of the information they had accumulated and emailed his report to the email address he had been given in the dossier. "Jonah, I think you should head to Malibu in the morning to check out the movie producer," said Brock, "while the we start to track down Mr. Kholi."

Jonah answered with a quick, "Roger that."

As the team broke up for the night, Brock shook hands with Roxy, then Jonah, and said, "Good work, team. Now, let's call it a night and get back at it early in the morning."

That evening, Athena checked her email and read over the update she had received from Brock. Immediately the information regarding the Palo Verde nuclear site caught her eye. She remembered that the guys in the hall had discussed an electronic magnetic pulse and how they would either need nuclear material or a huge power source for their mission; Palo Verde provided both. She scanned the information regarding the two men and was satisfied that her crew was adequately covering the situation. She sent an *email received* confirmation to Brock and turned her attention to Palo Verde.

She started scouring the Internet, looking specifically for sites and blogs that mentioned Palo V. Athena went from site to site for hours, copying information that she felt would be relevant.

Meanwhile, her wide and constant Internet activity had caught the attention of Abdul Amir, a mid-level Al Qaeda operative in Saudi Arabia.

After all of the time Athena had spent online, she had forgotten to mask her IP address with the VPN. She knew what a VPN did, but in her normal life she was never really concerned about that kind of privacy.

Every computer that connects to the Internet has a unique address, much like a house on a street. An IP (Internet Protocol) address is a series of four numbers, each one ranging from 0 – 255; each of the series of numbers is separated by a period. An example of what most IP addresses would be something like *127.0.0.1*. A sophisticated hacker can track an IP address right down to the exact location where the computer is being used.

Unbeknownst to Athena, she had just told the bad guys where she lived.

It was late, but Athena texted Rocker and Peanut to let them know that she would give them an update in the morning. She replied to

Brock's email with a message that read, *Proceed. Possible EMP,* and then was off to bed.

The next morning, Jonah got up early to catch a flight to Malibu that he booked on Priceline the previous night. He carefully packed everything he needed, including a special gun that he had purchased when he was in the CIA. The gun was 3D-printed of a carbon nanofiber material and would not show up on metal detectors; he packed it strategically into a secret compartment of his carry-on bag.

When he arrived to go through the security gate, he removed his shoes and belt and placed his laptop in one of the grey bins provided. He walked into the big scanner and raised his hands over his head as he was checked for weapons. As his bag moved through the scanner, the x-ray technician motioned to a supervisor. "Is this your bag?" the supervisor asked Jonah.

Relaxed, Jonah replied. "Yep. That's mine." The supervisor moved the bag over to a side table so he could get a better look at what might have caught the attention of the other officer.

Jonah had been in this situation many times and did not let the routine bag check rattle his nerves. After only a few moments and a brief inspection, the security supervisor looked up at Jonah and said, "Have a great day, sir."

"Will do."

The plane took off on time and the flight was extraordinarily ordinary. Jonah arrived in Malibu as planned and on schedule.

An hour passed before Brock reached out to Roxy.

"How long will it take for you to get into the TSA (Transportation Security Administration) system without being noticed?" he asked his new tech expert.

"I think it will take a few hours, but I'll know more once I get in to the system," she responded.

"We need to track down this guy Kholi before things go south."

"I know," said Roxy. "It might take a while, but I'll get the information."

"Roger that. Go get 'em," Brock ordered.

"I'm on it." She turned her attention away from her phone and back to her laptop, reached for her Wi-Fi card and switched on her VPN.

It took most of the day, but Roxy did her usual computer magic and hacked into the FAA logs. They showed that Kholi had flown from Denver to Detroit and was booked on a flight to India the next morning. She immediately emailed the information to Brock.

Brock reached in his pocket to pull out his phone, having felt the familiar buzz indicating that an email had arrived. He quickly reviewed the message and, after a couple of taps with his fingers, put the phone to his ear. "Hey brother," said Brock. "It's me. I need a favor."

The voice on the other end responded, "What's up?"

Brock continued. "I've got something brewing and I need to hold up a suspect. Can you place him on 'The List?' I need to slow him down."

The List refers to the *terrorist watch list* which was created following the terrorist attacks in New York, Washington, DC and Pennsylvania on September 11, 2001. Once someone has been placed on the watch list, it becomes very difficult to fly on a commercial plane, and it is also near impossible to get your name off the list. So what Brock was asking for was no small favor.

A second or two passed before the other voice on the phone finally said, "You still owe me from the last favor." Brock was feeling a little nervous before he heard, "Yeah, I guess. Who ya got?"

"Suspect's name is Farhan Kholi," Brock replied, proceeding to give his friend all of the relevant details.

Once finished with the call, Brock reached back out to Roxy. "One thing is for sure; our friend Mr. Kholi won't be going anywhere soon," Brock told her. "I'll head out to Detroit and see what's up with him."

"Alright, I'll continue to follow up on the other leads from here," Roxy answered, hanging up the phone.

With the boys busy on their own duties, Roxy decided to focus her attention on the girl that was in the service hall while the suspects were passing through.

Chapter 9

JEOPARDY

Al Qaeda has cells all over the United States. Most of these cells are lone individuals or small groups that usually work without instruction from anyone. After watching the flurry of searches for information about Palo Verde stemming from Colorado, Abdul Amir sent an email to an associated operative that was in the Denver area; the message read in Arabic: *Check out Lakeview, CO - 121.56.28.115.*

The note found its way to Muhammad Ali Aziz, a 22-year-old Pakistani student in the United States on an international student visa to study engineering at the University of Colorado.

He spoke very good English with only a slight accent. He wore short dark hair and a beard and typically dressed in blue jeans and a T-shirt with sandals; even in Colorado, he resisted giving up his comfortable sandals, to which he had become so accustomed in Pakistan.

It was mid-morning by the time Aziz checked his email. He almost missed the message, as it had been delivered to his junk mail folder, but on this day, he checked to see what might be there.

Aziz opened the newest email that didn't have a subject and read, *Check out Lakeview, CO - 121.56.28.115.*

Aziz was using a high-end PC laptop, fully loaded with all of the bells and whistles. He connected it to the Internet using his VPN and opened up a network utility program that let him track IP addresses. He punched in the number that was on the message and tracked it back to its Internet service provider (ISP). After a few more strokes on his keyboard, he had what he needed. He shut down his computer, grabbed his backpack, and headed out. He punched the address that he had retrieved into the built-in GPS of his cargo van and drove about forty-five minutes ... to Lakewood.

It was around 3:00pm when Steve Miller arrived home. He had left work early, feeling guilty that he hadn't spent enough time with his family since he forced them to move across the country. Sarah and Mikey were home, but Jeanie was out with Jimmy and Annie.

He entered the front door and threw his car keys on the entry table. He yelled, "Sarah, I'm home!"

Sarah grabbed Mikey and went to greet her husband. "What are you doing home?" she asked.

"I was feeling guilty; I've been gone so much, working so hard." As soon as he got the words out, there was a knock at the door. "You expecting anyone?" he asked.

"No. Is this one of your tricks?" Sarah smirked.

"Nope." Steve he headed to the door to see who was there.

Aziz had arrived at the address in question and found a new family from Washington, DC had just moved in. The new owner worked for a defense contractor. Recognizing that Steve was his likely target, he knocked on the front door and immediately poked a gun in Steve's face as it opened.

Aziz forced himself in and began to yell. "Get on the ground! Get on the ground!" Conveniently, he found everyone already gathered in the main living area just inside the front door. With everyone down, he bound Steve's hands behind his back with zip ties, then Sarah's, leaving the baby alone for the moment. He rifled through their pockets looking for cell phones and weapons.

"What do you want?!" Steve repeated. "What do you want?!" He kept asking. He felt it had something to do with his job; he had no idea they were here because of Jeanie. "Leave my family out of this!" Steve said, fearing for the safety of his wife and son.

"Shut up!" commanded Aziz.

The intruder quickly checked the other rooms in the house before returning to the living room. He pointed a gun at Sarah's head, "You. Get up."

Sarah couldn't breathe. She was crying … and scared.

"Okay. Alright," said Steve. "We're getting up. It's okay, babe. We're okay; just do what he says."

Aziz quickly ushered the three into his van and drove off.

Athena had heard the commotion from next door and she looked out the window, just in time to see her family being ushered into a white cargo van. She made a mental note of the license plate as the van rushed off.

Feeling lost, Jeanie impulsively ran outside, yelling at the van. "STOP! WHERE ARE YOU GOING?"

The vehicle drove away. Luckily for Jeanie, Aziz did not notice the young girl in his rearview mirror, screaming and chasing after him, or certainly Jeanie and her young friends would have been tied up and thrown into the back of the van as well.

Chapter 10

ALONE

R oxy went back to review the mall security footage, looking for any new information she could find about the girl who was hiding in the service hall. Looking at it all again, Roxy said to herself, "She has to be the one who called, based on the level of detail that we've been given." She watched as the cameras followed the girl out to the parking lot and into the Escalade.

She ran the plates and found the car was registered to Steve Miller, an engineer for NewG-Tech in Virginia. It wasn't long before she found the new address in Lakewood. She entered the address into the GPS on her iPhone and hurried out to her car.

As she opened the car door, Roxy activated the auto assistant on her phone and said, "Call Brock." As soon as the phone stopped ringing, she said, "It's Roxy."

"Whatcha got?" he replied.

"I've tracked down the girl from the mall security," she said. "I'm heading that way to review the situation."

"Roger that. Keep me up-to-date." *Click*.

It took Roxy about twenty minutes to make the drive to the Miller house. When she arrived, the front door was open and Roxy instinctively reached for her gun. She peeked in guardedly, only to find a girl in the middle of the living room crying and two other children trying to comfort her. Athena was sitting on the floor with her back against the wall. Her head was in her hands as she rocked back and forth, repeating out loud to herself, "What have I done? What have I done?"

Roxy slowly entered the house and quickly asked, "What's going on?"

Athena jumped up and gave her spy a hug. Rocker and Peanut stood there with their mouths open as Roxy walked through the door. Roxy was caught completely off-guard by the reaction of the kids; they seemed to *know* her.

She pushed Athena back from the hug and asked her, "Okay...what's going on here? What is happening? Who *are* you kids?"

Athena tried to choke back tears and answered, "They took my family. They took them!"

Roxy leaned over and held Athena with one hand on each arm and asked, "*Who* took them?"

Over the next several minutes, Roxy listened while *Athena* ... this not-yet-adolescent agent ... tried to explain the whole story to her.

"You kids did *all* of this*?*" their spy asked. "But how?" Amazed by everything she just heard she said, "I can't believe you kids were able to pull all of this off." She then proceeded to give her boss, *Athena*, an update.

"So, what do we do now?" Athena asked. Rocker and Peanut just stood there. They had believed their friend about the terrorists, but privately the siblings had discussed if there really was a possibly planned attack, and if so, what they could really do, if anything, about it anyway.

Athena composed herself as the group gathered around her. "At this point," Athena said, "I don't think we should brief Jonah or Brock about this."

"I agree," Roxy said. "It would be a distraction. They need to continue on their current missions; I'll brief them when it's appropriate."

Roxy took a deep breath...and stared at her three young clandestine colleagues. "Well, kids," she said, "I guess it is up to *us* to get your parents back!"

Athena smiled and ran to a closet that had already been retrofit with an electronic security lock. She punched in the combination, got the green light and opened the door. The closet, from the outside looked like any other door, but it was really the entrance to a hi-tech storage facility that held the latest research projects that Athena and her dad had been working on.

The door and the room had been installed by NewG-T before her family had arrived in Lakeview. Athena quickly looked over the collection of items and stuffed three of them in her backpack.

Roxy looked on with amazement as Athena grabbed her hand and said, "Let's go! I'll explain on the way."

Chapter 11

SUSPECTS

I t seemed like it took forever, but Jonah finally reached Malibu. He hopped into his rental car and headed to Frazier York's house. It took him around an hour and forty-five minutes to reach the house on Birdview. *Damn, I hate the traffic out here*, he thought to himself. Even so, he couldn't help but think that he was working his way through *one nice neighborhood*. He admired several extremely large homes nestled along the Malibu coast as he got closer to his destination.

When he reached the York house, the gate was open. He waited outside the large

Tuscan-style home for several minutes to get the lay of the land and took some photos with his camera phone.

Just as he was about to approach the house, Mr. York walked out of the front door. He got in his car, a black Audi TT convertible with tan leather seats, parked in the curved driveway in front of his house. The top was down, so Jonah got a good look at his suspect as he turned onto the street.

Using the S.O.P. (Standard Operating Procedure) when tailing a subject, Jonah let him pass by before putting his own car in drive, then quickly made a u-turn and followed York toward the interstate.

Jonah tailed him all the way to Hollywood. Again, all he could think was, *I hate this freaking traffic!* Nothing made him more furious than the monotony of sitting in traffic, but at least he wasn't alone; he had his suspect to keep him occupied. It was a long drive, but Mr. York finally reached his destination - Universal Studios.

Mr. York pulled up to the gate, showed his ID and eased up to the guard stand. Jonah watched as the security guard greeted his visitor. "Nice to see you, Mr. York," he said.

Jonah let York roll on through and waited a minute before pulling up to the gate himself. As he did, the security guard leaned out and said, "What can I help *you* with?"

Jonah reached into the breast pocket of his sports jacket and drew out his old FBI badge. "I need to ask you a few questions." No one is ever expecting a visit from an FBI agent, and it caught the guard off-balance ... which was Jonah's intention. "I need to ask you a few questions about Frasier York."

"Who?" The guard answered.

"Frasier York. The man you just let through the gate."

"I'm sorry, sir," stammered the guard. "I let hundreds of people through these gates each day. I just check their IDs and let 'em through. I don't know them. I mean, you know ... not *personally*."

"Alright, then. Let me through and I'll find someone who *does* know him."

"Yes, sir." A few seconds later, the guard allowed Jonah through to enter the studio property.

Back in Detroit, Brock decided to just wait on the concourse at the airport and watch for Mr. Kholi to arrive for his flight. His plan was to pose as a TSA (Transportation Security Agency) agent and interrogate the would-be terrorist. He waited there all day, and finally got his chance to grab his man as Kholi showed up at the counter to check in for his flight.

The ticket agent looked indifferently at the man in front of him and said, "Good afternoon. Can I get your driver's license?" He did this a thousand times a day, and since 2001, he had only seen two people approach his counter that were included on the terrorist watch list; both were mistakes.

His computer screen flashed a message that knocked him off-guard. It must have been obvious, because Mr. Kholi immediately began to feel uncomfortable. The ticket agent motioned for a supervisor and Brock moved in, flashing his fake TSA badge and directing airport police to usher Kholi into a secure room away from gate access.

Farhan Kholi was completely taken aback by this treatment. He was scared and couldn't understand what was happening. He was taken to a small room with one door and a two-way mirror. In the center was only a small wooden table with a matching chair on either side.

After getting the basics — name, address, destination, reason for travel, etc. — Brock started in with the tough questions. Brock was playing bad cop, bad cop and was doing a good job of playing both parts.

"Do you know Frazier York?" asked Brock.

Now Farhan was really confused. In a slow, uncertain voice, he replied. "Yeah ... he's a movie producer who lives in Malibu. I think."

Brock was going to have to push. "How do you know him? What were you doing in Lakewood? Where are you going? What do you know about Palo Verde? When is the last time you were in Arizona?"

Over and over, Brock peppered him with questions related to work, acquaintances, background, Palo Verde and nuclear materials. To say Kholi looked scared by this line of questioning is an understatement ... but there weren't many answers.

After more than an hour, Brock realized that he was barking up the wrong tree. He finally let Mr. Kholi leave and texted: that *apparently Kholi really was just a movie director, and he and York were scouting a location for their next terrorist action movie.*

Jonah got the text and had come to the same conclusion following his time spent with York.

During his interview, he was so scared. When he was confronted by Jonah and his 3D printed pistol he squealed like a little girl. Jonah asked virtually the same questions to Frasier York that Brock asked his suspect. But ultimately, he came to the same conclusion as Brock. These two were in the movie business and had no connection to Palo Verde.

Brock and Jonah figured it was time to regroup and initiated a conference call with Roxy via their cell phones; she answered immediately.

"We have a situation here," Roxy said. "I need you both to head to Palo Verde. We'll meet you there." Then the call dropped.

Simultaneously, as if on cue, Brock and Jonah said in unison: "Did she say *we*?"

Chapter 12

THE HUNT

R oxy didn't know for sure where the bad guys were taking Athena's family, but she felt it was a safe bet that they would be heading towards Palo Verde. So Roxy, Athena, Rocker and Peanut piled into her vehicle and hit the road.

Athena reached into her backpack and pulled out one of the items that she had pulled from "the closet." Holding a small square device in her hand, she held it up and said, "This thing can track the GPS coordinates of any cell phone just by punching in the phone number assigned to it."

She punched in her dad's number and an image showed up on the screen in a 3D hologram; the markings representing her family seemed to be moving southeast.

Roxy looked over to Athena and stepped on the gas in an effort to catch up with her family. "Don't worry," she said. "We'll get your family back." Athena looked at her hopefully, but she wasn't as confident.

Once they were on the road, Roxy called a friend in the FBI, gave him the plate number of the van that Athena had made a point to remember just an hour earlier, and drove as fast as she could to catch up with her family.

Aziz had driven about seventy miles and pulled off the main road to a small field where there was a helicopter waiting for him. He opened the side door of the van in which Steve, Sarah and Mikey were restrained. "Get out of the van!" he shouted as he grabbed Steve by the arm and dragged him from the van. Sarah and

Mikey followed them as Aziz stood beside the white cargo van looking at a black helicopter.

Once they were out of the vehicle, two men who looked Middle Eastern headed toward them. They escorted Steve and his family to the helicopter, and having offloaded his cargo, Aziz headed home.

The helicopter's blades began to spin as hoods were placed over the heads of Steve and his family. They were each injected with a sleep agent and loaded onto the helicopter ... and they were off.

Chapter 13

FAST GETAWAY

———————————

Since being kidnapped from their house in Lakewood, Steve and Sarah had been bound and gagged, trapped in the back of a van that was carrying them to ... wherever their final destination might be. They sat quietly, not wanting to give their captors any reason to do them harm. At least for now, Steve believed they were not yet in imminent danger; if they had been, he surmised, they would already be dead. He continually looked to his wife in hopes of heartening her and easing her fear.

Sarah was terrified by the ordeal, but Steve's calmness did help to reassure her that they would be okay. She was glad the long ride in the van had caused little Mikey to fall asleep, and she worried what a crying toddler would do to the attitude of their captors.

They weren't sure how long they were in the van, but Steve could see the helicopter as they approached. They were brusquely hustled from one vehicle to another, and before they could really get their bearings, everything went black.

Steve, Sarah and Mikey were already unconscious by the time the helicopter took off. It appeared to be a holdover from the Vietnam era. It was black and it had two sliding doors, similar to those in a minivan. Two men rode in the cockpit, and two remained in the back along with the hostages.

Steve slowly began to gain consciousness. He knew, *he thought,* he was flying. He sat still, pretending to be asleep, trying to figure out what was happening and why. He was sure it had something to do with his job as a weapons designer, and he wondered how his abductors found him and why they had abducted him and his family.

He also thought about Jeanie. He hoped she was safe and wondered what she would she do when she realized that they were gone. As he laid there, a man with a machine gun started to poke him in his side.

"Wake up! Wake up!" the man said with a heavy Middle Eastern accent. "Who are you? What is your name?"

Still foggy from the drugs, Steve struggled to understand the question. "Steve Miller," he replied. "I'm Steven Miller."

"Who do you work for?"

Steve didn't answer.

"*Who* do you *work* for?" his captor repeated.

"I work for Wal-Mart," said Steve.

"Liar! Who do you work for? CIA? FBI? NSA?"

"I don't know what you're talking about."

The terrorist hit Steve on the head with the barrel of his gun. "Liar!"

With all the commotion, Sarah came to and made eye contact with Steve. He closed his eyes hard as if to say, "Pretend to sleep."

She understood what he meant and laid there quietly. She could feel Mikey lying next to her and could tell he was breathing. She was scared but remained silent as they continued to question her husband.

"What do you know about Palo Verde?" they asked.

"Palo Verde?" Steve replied, more confused than ever. "I don't know what you're talking about. Why have you taken us?"

"Liar!" The frustrated interrogator yelled as he smacked Steve again on the head with the butt of his gun, knocking him out. Sarah let out an audible gasp as she watched her husband fall to the floor. Still feeling the effects of the drugs, she soon passed out again as the helicopter continued to its destination.

Having finished the journey, the helicopter began to hover over a landing pad just inside the gates of a military complex. A flurry of activity ensued as several men dressed in military fatigues began to converge on the aircraft.

The pilot looked over his shoulder as the ground crew entered the side doors. "Take them below!" he commanded as the propeller began to slow. "Take the man for interrogation, and tie up the woman; we may need her as leverage." The ground crew dragged Steve and his family off the helicopter and took them to an underground military facility.

Chapter 14

THE CHASE

As the helicopter began to take off, Athena immediately noticed something different happening to the coordinates on her GPS device.

"Roxy, look!" Athena said, as she showed the device to Roxy. "This was designed to work as a targeting system for a new missile that could target anyone in the world by their cell phone number," Athena told the group. The idea was Athena's, but her dad ended up taking most of the credit.

She showed the coordinates to Roxy. "They're flying, most likely by helicopter," she said. Amazed by the technology Athena held in her hand, all Roxy could say was, "Incredible."

They drove through the night and stopped in Phoenix to catch up with the boys.

Sarah and Mikey were taken into a small room with no windows and only one door. Sarah was bound, blindfolded and gagged, and Mikey was placed in a makeshift playpen. Steve was also blindfolded while his hands remained bound with zip ties.

The men surrounding them all spoke Arabic. Steve understood much of what they were saying, as he had spent nearly two years in Saudi Arabia during the first Gulf War. They pressed him, asked about his work and why he was trying to track their movements over the Internet. Despite his seemingly convincing denials, the terrorists just wouldn't believe him.

The next morning Brock, Jonah, Roxy and the kids met at Waffle House for breakfast. Athena, concerned for her family, was ready to get going. "Come on, guys. Let's go..." she implored.

"Hold on," Brock said. "Roxy, what's the sitrep?"

Sitrep is military slang for the situational account of an area or mission.

Roxy replied, "We have an unknown number of hostiles and three hostages. We've tracked their location by cell phone pings with tech provided by our employer, Athena."

Brock and Jonah looked at each other with utter disbelief with that bit of information — but remained quiet for the rest of the briefing.

Roxy continued, "We believe the group is planning an EMP out of Palo Verde, and it appears to be well-funded and organized." She continued, "I know you have questions regarding our employer, but I'll have to bring you up to speed at a later time."

After the briefing, they paid the check, loaded up into two SUVs, and headed out.

Luckily, the bad guys did not turn off Steve's cell phone. The GPS could still track it, and the coordinates on the device confirmed their location as just outside Palo Verde. It was only about twenty miles to their destination; Roxy grabbed her walkie, clicked the button and said, "Brock, twenty miles to target."

"Roger that," the walkie squawked back.

Satellite imagery showed that there was only a clear line of sight from the facility to where Athena's family was being held to the road that led to the facility. "Let's stop two miles short and walk to minimize our visibility."

The imagery provided by Athena's tech, as well as Google maps, revealed the location to be an abandoned military facility that was used as an ICBM (Intercontinental Ballistic Missile) launch facility during the Cold War.

During the height of the Cold War, the U.S. had ICBM silos scattered all across the country in case a thermonuclear war broke out with the USSR (Union of Soviet Socialist Republics). This number dwindled during the Clinton presidency. Through diplomatic efforts, the U.S.A. had reached an agreement with Russia to reduce missile stockpiles with the fall of the former Soviet Union. As a result, missile silos that once housed very destructive weapons ... were now empty.

Athena rummaged through her backpack for the other two devices she had grabbed from the closet.

One was about the size of a large TV remote control. This was a serious weapon with two settings. The first setting carried a sonic pulse along a fine laser. The frequency could be set to cause confusion or even to disrupt a heartbeat.

The second setting was a high-intensity laser that could cut through quarter-inch steel at short distances.

The other item was a super-sensitive unidirectional microphone that was only a bit bigger than a hearing aid. This microphone was sensitive enough to hear a conversation through a cinder block wall located almost one hundred feet away.

Jonah and Brock went ahead of the group to do a little recon. Both men were laying on their bellies, looking through a pair of high-powered binoculars. "I've got two guards at the gate in U.S. military fatigues," Jonah said as Brock scanned the perimeter for additional guards.

"The perimeter is clear," Brock replied.

"It looks like a typical military facility except for what appears to be an elevator," Jonah reported.

"Looks like their goal is to make it appear as though the army was moving to reopen the facility," Brock whispered to Jonah.

"I wonder how much of the complex is underground," Jonah replied.

"Based on the size of the elevator, I'm guessing there is a large subterranean facility," Brock answered.

It was almost as if a light bulb went on over Athena's head. "I have a plan!" she said in a voice just above a whisper. "We could commandeer an ambulance and use the sonic pulse from the pulse generator I brought to give one of the guards heart problems."

"It can do that?" Roxy asked.

"Absolutely!" She continued. "The pulse generator uses a micro, high-powered sonic..."

"Hold on, Athena. We don't need to know all of the science behind the device. Just as long as it works."

"Oh, it will work, and that guard won't know what hit him."

"Boy, she scares me," Rocker said to his sister. The group kind of nodded and had a little laugh together.

Even with all of the danger around her, Athena took a breath and felt content and secure around her friends. This was something new for her. In her past life at her old school, she never had close friends. She was proud to be part of this group, even after only a short time together.

Athena continued to relay her plan. "Once the guard falls ill, let's hope they'll call for an ambulance, and not just let him die or kill him. Assuming they call an ambulance, we can intercept it here and disable the other guard once on site. If they go for the other option, we'll have a diversion and one less guard for the boys to deal with."

Suddenly the grown-up spies were glad to have Athena along. "Rocker, you and Peanut need to be bait in order to get the ambulance to stop before the gate. Roxy, you need to stay with them, and once the ambulance stops, just do your thing. I'll move forward with Brock. And Jonah, I'll need you to intercept their call and let us know what they are deploying to the scene."

"Roger that!" Jonah said enthusiastically.

Brock and Athena moved into position to use the pulse generator portion of the device. Jonah pulled out a cell phone repeater which would enable him to scan signals coming to and from nearby cell towers. Roxy waited by the car with Rocker and Peanut, just in case an ambulance really did show up.

Roxy reached for the walkie and pressed the button as she spoke into the mouthpiece. "Everyone in position?"

"Roger that," Brock replied as he looked over to Athena. "You ready?"

Athena nodded and turned her attention to the pulse generator. "Yep, I'm ready." She looked through the built-in sight, which showed the directional laser otherwise invisible to the eye.

Which one of these guys is about to have a bad day? Athena thought to herself. "Eenie, Meenie, Miney, Mo," she whispered.

Brock looked at his boss and smirked. He couldn't help but think that this was one of the best gigs he had ever been assigned. He thrived in dangerous situations, but he felt like he was actually having fun.

It didn't take long for the unfortunate recipient of Athena's pulse generator to grab for his chest. After a few seconds, the other guard realized his partner was in distress, and instinctively he reached for his cell phone and dialed 9-1-1.

Jonah was able to intercept the call as he listened to their communication. The team was in luck; an ambulance had been dispatched.

He looked over to Roxy and gave her the thumbs-up sign.

She pulled her SUV over to the side of the road about half a mile from their current location. She opened up the hatch and scattered some of their supplies on the ground. "Rocker, you come lay down over here and I will stand by you. Peanut, you stand by the road to flag down the ambulance, and when they come to help, I'll hit them with my taser. Then we can take the ambulance and rendezvous with the rest of the team."

The game was underway.

Chapter 15

THE RESCUERS

The team waited for what seemed like an hour, but it was only between ten and fifteen minutes before the ambulance arrived. As the siren warned of the vehicle's approach, Peanut ran to the side of the road and started to jump up and down, waving her arms high above her head.

As predicted, the paramedics pulled to the side of the road. The driver reached for a hand-held radio transmitter to report that they had stopped to assist a family on the side of the road.

"My brother was bitten by a snake!" yelled Peanut as the paramedics got out to help. As they rushed to the back of the ambulance and turned to grab their bags, Roxy zapped them from behind with the taser.

"Sorry about this boys, but we need to borrow your ambulance," Roxy said to the unconscious medics, then turned back to the kids. "I'll zip-tie their hands and feet, gag 'em and leave them in the back."

She knew this was risky, but it was a chance they would have to take; she wanted to keep them safe. "I'll be able to explain this once we're clear of danger," she told Rocker and Peanut. Then she reached for her walkie and alerted their partners. "We're en route."

Brock replied, "Roger that." He looked over and nodded to Athena. "Grab your gear. We're out of here."

As they were approaching their vehicles, Roxy and the kids came rolling up in the ambulance. "You guys need a ride?" she said with a wink. Athena smiled and the two piled into the back. Once in, they drove a little further to pick up Jonah, who was doing some additional recon of the gate.

"What's the sitrep?" Brock asked.

"One guard down and three guards standing around him," Jonah responded. He and Brock quickly began to swap clothes with the paramedics as the group of spies rolled towards the outpost where they believed Athena's family was being held.

One of the guards opened the gates as the ambulance approached and waved them through. "I'll go left, and you go right," Brock said to Jonah.

"Roger that." The two quickly piled out through the back doors of the emergency vehicle, surprising and then disabling the remaining guards. The rest of their group shot out of the van, ready to rescue Athena's family and prevent a terrorist attack on the U.S.

Athena reached for her tracking device. She stood still, turning only at her waist from left to right as she tried to get a signal. "They're here," she said as she looked at the tracking device. "The signal is weak. I'm guessing they are about fifty feet below."

The commotion at the gate sounded an alarm which alerted the rest of the bad guys. Over the blaring horns, Brock shouted, "Well, I guess we'll have to do this the hard way!"

Jonah, Brock, and Roxy all pulled guns from their holsters. Jonah and Brock took the stairs while Roxy and Athena headed towards the elevator roughly forty yards in front of them.

The elevator was risky business; there was surely a surveillance camera inside, and trying to walk down ten flights of stairs undetected didn't seem like a great option. They made it only two stories before the elevator stopped.

"Crap!" Athena exclaimed. She and Roxy looked at each other, and Athena held one finger up as if to say, "One second." She pulled the laser from her pocket and handed it to Roxy.

"Here. Use this," said Athena.

"How does it work?" Roxy asked, inspecting the device.

"You need to switch the laser to 'cut' and then press the button on the top. It works best if you keep the laser at least ten inches away from the surface you're cutting.

"And ... ummm ... make sure not to point it at any reflective surfaces. I wouldn't want you to cut a hole through either of us," Athena said jokingly as Roxy gave a concerned look. Athena smiled and gave her a wink. Roxy still wasn't sure if Athena was kidding about reflective surfaces, but she was careful to avoid them as she pointed the laser towards the ceiling.

It didn't take long before Roxy had cut an eighteen-inch square in the ceiling of the elevator. As the large square hit the floor, she squatted down and cupped her hands in front of her knees.

"Come on, I'll give you a boost," she said, first boosting up Athena and then pulled herself up and through. Once on top of the elevator, they scanned the elevator shaft. It was dimly lit, and about every ten feet above and below there was a cutout for elevator door access. There were rails that guided the elevator and an umbilical cord that housed electricity and data cables.

Roxy pointed to the access ladder. "Here. We'll take this down the rest of the way." Athena was feeling a little nervous, but she knew there was no other way down.

"Hold on!" Athena said to her partner, pulling a range-extending transmitter from her bag that would switch between radio frequencies and voice of internet protocol (VoIP). "We'll need this to communicate with the surface once we're underground."

"Okay, then," Roxy answered. "Got anything *else* in there? I think it's better than my purse." The levity helped to ease Athena's nerves as they headed down the ladder.

At the bottom, Jeanie checked the GPS and buzzed Jonah and Brock to give them the coordinates. Athena and Roxy got into position. Jonah and Brock geared up — each complete with an assault rifle, pistols, several loaded magazines, a tactical vest and an assortment of flash and smoke grenades.

Brock and Jonah headed down the stairs. They were on their way to catch up with the girls. With typical military precision they scanned the halls, checking each door as they worked their way through the building. It was as if the two had worked together for many years.

Room-by-room they entered yelling, "Clear!" as each was secured. The commotion they made sounded like twenty men working their way through the building.

As Jonah and Brock worked their way down, terrorists began to move in on their positions. They reached the bottom floor and found the room where Sarah and Mikey were being held. They could hear men yelling in Arabic, coming down the hall toward them.

Brock scanned the room. Sarah was tied up and gagged, and Mikey was still in his makeshift playpen. Jonah monitored the hall. "Contacts left!" he yelled as footsteps became louder and louder. Brock made eye contact with Sarah.

"We're going to get you out of here, but first I need you to stay still and be quiet." She blinked and nodded, acknowledging his command.

The two spies took up position by the door. "I go high and you go low," Brock calmly said to Jonah in a near whisper.

Without saying another word, Jonah pulled a flash grenade from his tactical vest, pulled the pin and tossed it down the hall. Once they heard the explosion, they leaned out of the doorway where Mikey and Sarah were being held captive. There was a lot of noise and commotion, and then it went strangely silent. Sarah could hear the men yell, "Clear left! Clear Right!" as the two well-trained men moved in sync with one another and disabled hostile targets one after another.

Once the gunfire began to ring out, both Roxy's and Athena's eyes grew wide as they looked at each other. Roxy's first thought was about keeping Athena safe. "Let's hide in here," she said to her young partner, grabbing her by the arm and pulling Athena behind her into the dark room.

Athena was shaken. She worried about her parents and her brother. With all they had been through, the loud gunfire made this whole event seem less like a game; this was *real*.

Up until now, Athena had not really worried about her own safety. She had confidence in her team, never questioning that they would be able to bring everyone home, safe and sound.

Up until now.

Roxy could sense her fear. She reached out her hand to touch Athena's. "We're going to make it. I promise."

Jonah and Brock continued to scan the hallway. Brock took a deep breath, as if to say, "Whew. I'm glad that's over." He locked eyes with Jonah and took his first and middle fingers, pointing to his own eyes then down the hall.

Jonah stepped over the bodies of terrorists as he remained in a half-crouched position, assault rifle ready to fire. He moved slowly down the hall, checking every door, while Brock searched the bodies for additional information about the terrorist's plans.

Amid the sudden quiet, Roxy reached for her walkie, pushed the button and whispered, "Can I get a sitrep?"

While Brock worked the gruesome process of searching through dead terrorists, he reached for his walkie to reply. "We're on the bottom floor with a number of dead hostiles. Mother and brother secured. Jonah is assessing remainder of the threat. You can join us in room 1024."

Athena's body relaxed a bit as she heard the report, and they began to converge on their position. "What about *Dad?*" she gasped as she looked up to Roxy with a concerned look.

"Honestly, I feel he is okay," Roxy replied.

Steve had been taken to a room on the other end of the complex from his family. His hands were bound over his head around a pipe that ran across the top of the room, leaving him hanging. His socks and shoes had been removed, but he still had the rest of his clothes on.

One very muscular man stood in front of him. He was taping his knuckles, much like an

MMA fighter. There was another man keeping watch at the door and armed with a machine gun.

A third man seemed to be keeping watch over the first two; he was in charge. He was wearing a nicely tailored suit and expensive shoes. He looked Middle Eastern, but he had a British accent.

"Why are you here, Mr. Miller?" he asked politely.

Steve looked up at the man, "I have no idea. Why have you taken my family and me? I'm a salesman for a tech company. What could you possibly want with me?"

"Come now, Mr. Miller … we will find out what we need to know." The nicely dressed man looked towards the muscle man and gave him a nod. On cue, he punched Steve in the gut. There was an audible "Ooof!" as the force of the punch forced the air out of Steve's lungs. "One way or the other."

Just as he was about to ask his second question, gunfire was heard in the distance. With a surprised look on his face, he shouted orders in Arabic to the guard at the door and the muscle man. There was some chatter back and forth. The muscle man grabbed a gun that was propped up against the wall.

Steve looked as if he had been in a car wreck. The terrorists had roughed him up a good bit, even before his interrogation had begun. The well-dressed man looked Steve up and down. "Well, well," he said. "That is certainly a prompt rescue operation for a simple *salesman*."

Steve really didn't know who might be there to rescue him and he certainly would be surprised to learn that his brilliant young daughter orchestrated the whole thing.

The well-dressed man began to pat Steve down. "Where is it?" he asked.

"Where's what?"

"The tracking device. I know you have one on you. How else would they have found you so quickly?"

"There is no device! I don't know what you want! Leave me alone!" As the well-dressed man continued to pat him down, Steve knew that he had to take the opportunity of being alone and so close to his captor to try to escape.

With a surprisingly lucky and swift move, Steve pulled his legs up from the waist and wrapped them around his captor. He conveniently caught him around his arm and shoulder, leaving one arm over his head with his forearm suck against his ear. Steve began to squeeze his thigh muscles with all of his might.

With that one move, the tide had turned. The well-dressed man squirmed, fought and then ... *relaxed*.

Steve held on and continued to squeeze for an extra minute to make sure his captor would not get back up. When he finally let go, the man in the suit slumped to the floor. Athena's father then looked around the room to see if he could find a way to free himself from the pipe to which he was bound.

The room looked almost like a utility room. There were no windows and only the one door. There was a desk with a computer, a chair, and a four-drawer filing cabinet. Strewn around the room were a lot of letter-sized pieces of paper and a briefcase.

As he looked around the room, Steve noticed his shoes were tossed to the side of the cabinet. He could not help but wonder whether or not his family was safe.

Steve noticed how quiet the facility had suddenly become. The commotion had settled, almost unnervingly so. Should he call for help? Maybe not. He didn't necessarily want the terrorists to come back and find the well-dressed man lying on the floor.

What else can I do? he thought to himself. *Without a key or bolt cutters, I'll never get off this dang pipe.*

Out of options, Steve started yelling.

"HELP! HELP! I'M IN HERE! I'M IN HERE!" he yelled. He waited for a minute to see if he could hear any response, and yelled again.

Please God. Please help me, he thought.

Roxy and Athena were working their way down to the guys when Athena noticed a large device with a radioactive symbol sticker on its side. She recognized it right away from all of her work on targeting systems.

"Holy crap!" she said out loud as she stopped in her tracks. She stood there looking at the box in near disbelief.

Roxy stopped and looked over to her young partner. "What is it?" she asked, turning her gaze to see what Athena had noticed. Instantly

Roxy could feel the fear rise in her as she looked at the box with the nuclear symbol.

"Do you know what this is?" Athena asked.

Roxy nodded. "Yes, this is a warhead for an intercontinental ballistic missile." This one appeared to contain nuclear material.

"Wait, Roxy!" Athena shouted. "These guys have a real nuke; you've gotta help me disarm it!"

Roxy reached for her walkie. There was the expected static as she initially hit the button to speak. "Brock, can I get a copy?" She wanted to make sure he was listening before she relayed the news regarding the device.

"Copy that, Roxy," he said as he turned from his task of searching another terrorist.

Roxy looked over to Athena as she relayed the next bit of information. "Brock, we have located the TNW." This is a military acronym for *Tactical Nuclear Weapon*. While the team knew there was the possibility of a nuke, they hadn't really been prepared to find one, especially one that could be *armed*.

Jonah was headed back to Brock's location as the news came across the walkie. He could see the concern on Brock's face as he approached.

"What's up?" Jonah asked.

"We have a situation here," he replied.

Sarah could see the men talking in the hall, but she could not hear what they were saying. "Hey! Will somebody untie me here?" she yelled from her chair.

Brock and Jonah looked in her direction and continued talking without giving her any additional acknowledgement. "The girls have located a TNW," said Brock. Jonah turned white, and this concerned Sarah.

"Armed?" responded Jonah.

"At this point we don't know. The girls are examining the device. If the facility is secure, you need to take the woman and the kid to the surface. Take the ambulance, Rocker and Peanut, and get to a minimum safe distance."

"What about the girls?"

"We may need Athena to disarm the device. So, for now, I'll stay behind with them for as long as I can. When we're done, we'll take the helicopter — if it's still here — and meet you at your location."

"Roger that," Jonah said as he started to walk back to the room where Sarah was tied up. He put his hand on Brock's shoulder as if to say, *"Good luck."*

As he went in to get Sarah and Mikey, Brock reached for his walkie. "I'm on my way. What's your twenty?"

A few seconds later, Brock received his reply. "Checking." Roxy looked at Athena. Where the heck *are* we?" She moved back from the device to look around.

"Looks like we're one floor above you, close to room 978."

"Roger that. I'm on my way," said Brock.

Jonah turned to walk towards Sarah, who gave him a piercing stare. Her stare was so intense, it made him uncomfortable. Somehow, he knew that Athena's father had seen that look before.

"I'm Jonah. We are part of a team that was put together to rescue you and your family," he explained as he moved to the back of her chair, untying her hands. He reached for a knife that was in his waistband. With a swift move, he pulled up the knife, flipped it over in his hand, and cut the electrical ties that were binding her hands like he had done a thousand times before.

Freed, Sarah moved her arms forward and massaged one with the other. "Thank you," she said, continuing to rub her wrists.

She moved over to the makeshift playpen where Mikey was sleeping. "Oh, thank God," she said aloud as she picked up her son. "Have you seen Steve?" she asked with a nervous voice.

"No ma'am, we have not located your husband yet, but the team is working their way through the facility. We'll find him."

"Do you think he's alright?"

Jonah looked at her and nodded. "We'll find him. I'm sure he's okay. First, I have to get you two to the surface to ensure your safety. I'll be able to give you more details once I know you and your son are safe."

He didn't know for sure that Steve was safe, but he had to get the two to a safe distance. "Stay behind me," Jonah said, reaching for the rifle that hung from his shoulder by its strap. He checked his magazine to see how many rounds he had left, then proceeded to lead Sarah and Mikey to the elevator. Together they carefully worked their way around the perimeter of the building towards the exit.

As they reached the elevator, Mikey was awake, alert, and looking around. He was clueless to the events that had brought them to this underground facility and the terrorists who abducted them from their home in Lakewood. The elevator door opened, and the three got on and headed to the surface.

Chapter 16

THE DEVICE

Brock started to work his way towards Roxy and Athena to check out the TNW. Rounding the corner to the stairwell, he heard someone yelling, "Help! Help! I'm in here!" This could be a trap. It was possible that one or more of the terrorists were using Steve to lure him into an ambush. If it *was* Steve.

He reached for his walkie. "Roxy? Roxy? You got a copy?"

"Yes, where are you?" she said intensely. "I've possibly located Mr. Miller, south stairwell. I need you to converge on my location ... use caution."

He stopped to check his ammo level. He had one flash grenade and two clips of 9mm for the HK MP5 assault rifle. For close quarter combat, he preferred his 1911 9mm pistol. He quietly pulled it from its holster and cocked it back to check the chamber, ensuring there was a bullet chambered. He turned the safety off with his thumb and held his position, waiting for backup.

Athena's eyes lit up with the news that her dad was alive. "Go get him. I'll stay hidden," she said.

"Roger that," Roxy said with a smile as she reached for her sidearm. She walked towards the south stairwell and spoke into her walkie, "On my way." She held her weapon at the ready, with both hands around the pistol grip, her arms extended and the barrel of the gun pointed down. She checked her corners as she worked her way towards the south stairwell.

As she got closer, she could hear Steve yelling for help. She quickly peeked around the corner to see if it was clear. She reached for her walkie. "Looks clear. Proceeding with caution."

With that word, Brock started up the stairs with his gun pointed in the direction he was walking, his eyes scanning meticulously from side to side. When he reached the top of the stairwell, he found Roxy waiting for him. He made eye contact and motioned his head to the right. She nodded approval and the two started to move quietly towards the yelling.

"Help! Come get me! I'm in here! Help..."

As they reached the door behind which Steve was being held, Brock reached for a flash grenade. Roxy shook her head to say "No," raising her gun. She silently mouthed, "High. Low," and Brock nodded in agreement. He moved back, giving Roxy the lower position as they entered the room.

As they came bursting into the room, they could see the well-dressed man on the floor and Steve hanging from the ceiling. "Clear! Clear!"

each of the spies yelled once they completed their scan of the room.

"Oh, thank God!" Steve said out loud as the two spies came to his rescue. Steve was weak from the hours spent hanging by his wrists. His arms and shoulders were sore and his throat was scratchy from all the yelling, but he was safe.

"Hello Mr. Miller, we're the rescue party," Roxy said with a smile.

Still in shock, Steve replied. "But who…"

"Never mind that right now." Brock cut in. "We have a situation. Your wife and son are safe and should now be at a minimum safe distance."

"Minimum safe distance?" Steve said in a shaky voice.

"Yes, sir. We believe we have an armed tactical nuclear weapon in the building. It is our working theory that the now-disabled terrorists were planning an underground blast to create a large EMP that would disable the power grid for the entire west coast.

"Holy cow! Whose theory exactly?"

"We'll get to that later. For now, we could use your expertise in disabling the device," Brock answered. Roxy grabbed Steve's elbow and started to lead the men to Athena and the device.

Roxy reported to Brock and Steve the situation with the device as they got closer. Rounding the corner, Roxy yelled, "Athena, you can come out!"

With those magic words, Athena appeared from her hiding place. Steve stopped mid-stride upon seeing his daughter, at which point Athena took off running, arms outstretched in front of her.

"Daddy!" she yelled as she ran into his arms. "Oh, Daddy! I was so worried about you and Mom!"

Steve was speechless. "But ... what? How? Wha...?" He stammered to find his words as he returned the biggest hug he had ever gotten. "Jeanie, what are you doing here?"

"Dad, I promise I'll explain everything. I promise. But first, we have a problem." She pointed to the nuclear warhead.

The device was approximately three and a half feet long and about eighteen inches across. The casing had already been removed, and it looked as if the terrorists had added a timer.

Jonah, Sarah and Mikey emerged from the elevator. Rocker nudged his sister, "Peanut, here they come."

As they got to the ambulance, Jonah looked to the two kids and the ambulance crew. "Good job, you two." He reached for his knife, "I'm going to cut you loose, but I think you should come with us. We need to get outta here in a hurry." The crew looked at him and shook their heads in agreement. "We'll get you to a place where you can get help, but unfortunately we're going to need your vehicle just a bit longer."

Rocker looked up, a little scared. "Where are Athena and Roxy?"

"They're safe," said Jonah. "Her dad, too. But right now, we've got to hightail it out of here; we'll catch up with them in a bit."

The group stood there in front of the warhead. "Yep, I'd say we have a problem," said Steve. "So, you think the plan was to create an EMP to disable the smart grid?"

"Yes, I tried to tell you," said Athena. "We stumbled across their plans online. I'm guessing that is why they took you and Mom."

"But who are *these* guys?" Steve asked, motioning to Roxy and Brock.

"Those are my spies."

Her dad raised his eyebrows. "*Your* spies? Uh-huh."

"Yeah. Jimmy, Annie and I hired them from Craigslist."

"Craigslist…spies. Okay," questioned Steve.

"It's true. Rocker and Peanut. I mean *Jimmy* and *Annie*. Rocker and Peanut are their spy names. My spy name is *Athena*."

"Athena. Okay."

"Dad, I promise, I'll tell you everything, but first can we disarm the thermonuclear device? What do you say?"

"Go find us some tools." He turned to Brock. "Wire cutters, screwdrivers, whatever you can find," Steve commanded.

"Roger that," Brock answered as he went on the hunt.

Steve stepped forward to get a closer look at the device. "This looks like an MIRV (multiple independently targetable reentry vehicle) from Cold War-era Russia. Unfortunately, when the Soviet Union fell, they really were not able to secure their weapons. Apparently, some made it out and onto the black market."

Steve's mind was turning over and over. "I think we'll need to take the nose cone off to get to the detonator." *How do we do that*, he thought. "I hope he can find us some tools."

Athena stepped next to her dad. Roxy sat back and observed the two as they deliberated as to how to disarm the bomb.

"I found some!" Brock yelled out as he returned from his search. He handed Steve a tool belt full of tools that he had discovered in one of the utility closets.

"Great work," Steve said, handing the belt to Athena. He looked down at his daughter, beaming with pride. "You've come this far. You've rescued your mom, me and Mikey. Now let's kick this bomb's butt and get home."

Athena looked up to her dad and smiled. "Roger that."

She dropped down to her knees in order to get a closer look. "Be careful," Roxy commanded as the two examined the device. Athena looked hard, top to bottom, examining every inch before making a move.

Then the timer clicked on. "Oh, crap!" shouted the girls in unison. Steve looked towards Athena; the timer showed five minutes ... *and counting*.

"They must have started it remotely. We've gotta call this in so we can evacuate the surrounding area, just in case," Steve said to the group.

Brock agreed. "I'll get to the surface, prep the helicopter and call a friend at the FBI. They'll need to be briefed. You guys just disarm that damn bomb."

With that, Brock shot towards the elevator.

Athena reached into her backpack, grabbed the listening device she'd taken from the closet earlier, and placed it in her ear. "Y'all be quiet. I want to hear every little sound when we take this thing apart."

Steve glanced over and offered a nervous smile as he watched his daughter reach into her bag and pull out the device with a laser cutter.

He carefully took the screws out of the nose cone and pulled it away from the casing, his hands shaking with tension. *Dude, chill. Be careful to not touch the housing*, he said to himself. As he removed the cone, he noticed there were two wires connecting the nose cone to the rest of the device.

"Don't move!" Athena shouted. "We can't break the connection from the cone yet."

She got down low, lying completely on her side. She pulled out her phone and turned on the flashlight. "Let me get a good look in there," Athena said. Both Steve and Athena looked hard over the device and the timer; they had to hurry.

"Three minutes," Roxy called out as the timer continued to count down.

Athena took a deep breath, looked at Roxy and then her dad, then turned her attention back to the device. "Looks like there is a fail-safe. If we try to defuse it from this end, we might just set the thing off by mistake. What do you think, Dad?"

Steve took another look inside the device from the front and nodded to his little girl.

"Two-fifteen." Roxy updated.

Having made it to the surface, Brock's first call was to an old FBI acquaintance. "James? Brock. Shut up and *listen*."

That got James' attention. It had been at least seven years since he had heard from Brock, and for those to be his first words ... something was *way wrong*.

"James, I'm at an abandoned base just outside Palo Verde. We have an armed TNW one hundred feet underground. I have a team actively trying to disarm the device right now. I need you to get your people to start evacuating the surrounding area just in case. I'll get you a full briefing later, assuming we make it out of here in one piece."

It took a second or two for James to absorb the information. "Okay, Brock ... I'm going to trust you on this one, but I'll look for a full debriefing when this is over."

"You got it, James. Thanks."

With that phone call behind him, Brock started for the helicopter that brought Steve and his family to this facility in the first place. He reached for his walkie and pressed the button as he spoke in to the handset.

"Jonah, you got a copy?"

"Copy that. I have Sarah, Mikey and the kids. We're headed west in order to get to MSD (minimum safe distance).

"Located Steve. He's no worse for wear. He and Athena are attempting to deactivate the device and Roxy will escort them topside once they make it."

"Roger that," Jonah answered as he looked over to see how Sarah was taking the news.

Oh, thank God, she thought as Rocker and Peanut started to high-five. Then Rocker had to ask.

"What device? What are they trying to disarm?"

Jonah took a deep breath and answered, "*Ummm*, we located a nuclear warhead that the terrorists had rigged with a timer. Athena and Steve — you heard him — are trying to disable the bomb before it ... before it *blows*."

A hush fell over the ambulance.

"One forty-five," Roxy shouted.

"Dad, I'm going to remove the side panel and see if we can get to the core without hitting the trigger. If we can do that, the device can explode without going nuclear."

"That's right," Steve answered. "If we can remove part of the compression core, there won't be enough compression to make the plutonium go to critical mass."

"One-thirty." Roxy continued her countdown.

Steve and Athena quickly worked to get the panel off and work their way to the core. "Roxy, give me your knife!" Athena commanded. Roxy handed it over, and Athena used the blade to peel back the casing and peer inside.

"There it is! Dad, I'll hold this panel back and you use her knife to remove a segment from the core without cutting any of the wires."

"Okay. Gently. *Gently*."

"One minute!"

Steve took a deep breath and slowly pried the segment off the core. "Got it, got it ... GOT it. Now RUN!"

The three took off running as fast as they could. "We've got to use the stairs!" Athena shouted. "The extra structure should protect us from the blast as we work our way out!"

They made their way up two flights of stairs before the blast shook the building. It was an enormously loud explosion, causing the foundation of the building to crack and turning off whatever electricity was left in the building.

Athena screamed as the building continued to shake and start to crumble. "Go! Go! Go!" Roxy yelled. "Keep going!" As they finally reached the surface, the stairwell collapsed beneath them.

The three fell to the ground exhausted. "We made it." Athena said breathlessly.

Roxy reached up to give Athena a high-five. "Geez, that was intense," Steve said out loud. Athena gave her dad another big hug, then turned to hug Roxy.

"I'm glad that's over," she said. "Did we really just stop a nuclear bomb?"

"Yes, you really did," Roxy said. "I'm so proud of you and what we were able to accomplish in such a short time. I've worked in intelligence for years, and I've never really saved the country until now."

The FBI had shown up in force to greet them as they reached the surface. Brock brought them up-to-speed as they began the cleanup.

"Athena, I want you to meet Field Director James Rawlings with the FBI," said Brock.

Athena extended her hand and said, "Nice to meet you. This is my dad, Steve Miller."

Director Rawlings gave Steve a nod. "You must be very proud of your girl here."

"Yes I am," he replied. "I've always been proud of her, but I'm not sure I want to know all of the details on this one."

Athena giggled. "No, Dad, you really don't."

Director Rawlings continued, "You did a good thing here, young lady, and I want to make sure you get a medal … even if no one can know. You've earned it. We'll need you to come to Washington so we can debrief you and your group."

It wasn't long before Jonah returned in the ambulance. As he pulled up to the gate, Brock came running up, "He's with us. Let him in." The guard at the gate waved him through. Once he came to a stop Sarah jumped out.

"Steve! Steve!" she yelled as she took off running to where he and Athena were getting checked out by the onsite medical crew. "Oh, my God, I was so worried! Are you alright?" she asked as she looked over all of Steve's cuts and bruises.

"Yeah, I'm fine, thanks to this girl right here." he said as he reached over and pulled Athena in for a big hug. As he did, Sarah broke down crying. Athena pulled her mom close so they all could get a great big family hug.

"Mom, we're fine. I was so scared that I'd never see you guys again. We had to do something. Most of the hard work was done by Brock, Roxy and the team."

Athena looked over to her team. "Mom, Dad, I'll be back," she said as she turned to walk back to the rest of her team gathered by the ambulance.

Athena and her spies, all formed a little circle and each started to place their hands towards the center as they gave the Musketeer chant: "All for one and one for all."

Director Rawlings leaned in to the group and gave them a wink. "I'll make sure you and your family get back to Denver in style." He waved for one of his men to take them to be debriefed and to the airport. "Brock, I'll need you and your team to stay behind to help fill in some of the info. Don't worry, Athena; no doubt you'll be seeing them again soon."

As the sun was setting in Palo Verde, the Millers, along with Jimmy and Annie, boarded a plane to head home.

The next morning, while the Millers were all still in bed, Jeanie's cell phone rang. She rolled over and reached out to her nightstand to answer it. The caller ID didn't display any name or number, but she decided to answer it anyway.

"Hello? Oh, uh, hi, Mr. President." She wiped her eyes and listened to the man on the other end of the phone. "Yes ... thank YOU Mr.

President," was all she said before hanging up the phone.

Until the next mission.

CPSIA information can be obtained
at www.ICGtesting.com
Printed in the USA
LVHW090314040220
645693LV00002B/319